UNTIL WE FALL

A FALLING NOVEL

JESSICA SCOTT

ALSO BY JESSICA SCOTT

THE FALLING SERIES

Before I Fall

Break My Fall

After I Fall

Catch My Fall

Until We Fall

The HOMEFRONT Series

Come Home to Me

Homefront

After the War

Find My Way Home

NONFICTION

To Iraq & Back: On War and Writing

The Long Way Home: One Mom's Journey Home From War

BOOKSHOTS

Dawn's Early Light

COMING HOME SERIES

Because of You

I'll Be Home For Christmas: A Coming Home Novella

Anything For You: A Coming Home Short Story

Back to You

Until There Was You

All for You

It's Always Been You

UNTIL WE FALL
A Falling Novel

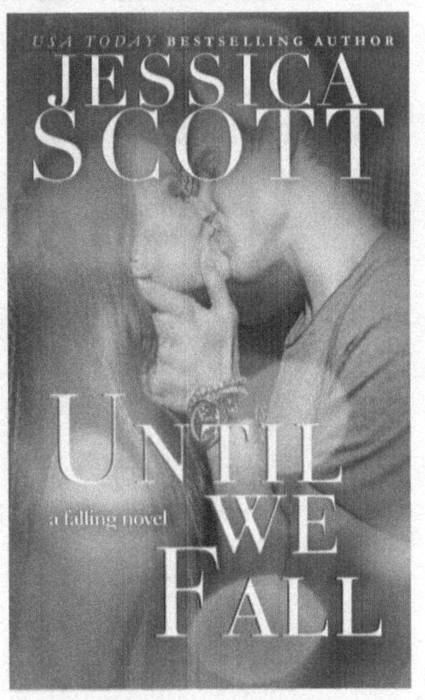

The darkness never forgets…
Caleb Gregory has spent ten years hiding in the dark,
refusing to speak about the night his young life was
destroyed. In his anger and his rage, he drank and fought
until he drove everyone away until he had no one left.

The light casts a long shadow…

Nalini King has devoted her post army life to her passion:
using yoga to heal her fellow soldiers. In doing so, she's
worked to forget the night her life burned down around her.

An unexpected storm…

When a storm forces them into the darkness together, these two wounded souls must face the demons of their past.

Because it is only in the darkest night that we can truly see the light.

THE FALLING SERIES
Before I Fall: Noah & Beth
Break My Fall: Abby & Josh
After I Fall: Parker & Eli
Catch My Fall: Deacon & Kelsey
Until We Fall: Caleb & Nalini

Note – these books are fiction. Any resemblance to real people or events is purely coincidence

Learn More At...
http://www.jessicascott.net
Follow Jessica on Twitter
Like Jessica on Facebook
Sign up for Jessica's Newsletter

PROLOGUE

Durham
Two Months Ago...

Caleb

When you hit rock bottom, there's really nowhere to go but up. Dragging your ass out of the hole you've fallen into isn't even the first step.

It's recognizing that you're in a hole in the first place.

Right now, I'm not in a hole, so I guess that's something. I'm up against a wall. One that's hard and cold and damp. Something stone, if the cold and damp pressing against my back are any indicators. Maybe brick. Possibly concrete. I'm not entirely sure.

"Comfortable?"

I blink hard but my eyes aren't working right. The light —and I'm not sure if it's daylight or street lamps or something else—feels like shards of glass piercing my retinas and stabbing my brain so I squeeze them shut again.

"Not really." At least, that's what I think I've said. My eyes are still refusing to work right, and those shards of glass that were just stabbing my eyes? Now they're trying to break out of the back of my skull.

"You need to get up."

That voice is rough. I frown and even that tiny gesture feels like it might kill me. Not that I've got a clue who the disembodied voice is attached to but then again, that's not really my problem, is it? I don't have to play nice.

I'm about this close to telling this dude to go fuck himself. Just as soon as I get my eyes working.

For some reason, "Rooster" by Alice in Chains starts playing in my head. They ain't killed me yet and all that, right?

"What time is it?"

That voice again. Fuck me, it's rough on the nerves. Oh wait. That one is mine.

"It's not about what time of day it is. It's about keeping your sorry ass out of jail."

Well, damn, that's got my attention. I summon the willpower to open my eyes. "What th'fuck are you talking about?"

I don't know who the man is in front of me. He's old enough to be my dad. At least, I think he is. I have deliberately had very minimal contact with the sperm donor over the last decade.

I've ignored the last few times he's called.

I don't even miss him.

I swallow a lump of something I'd rather not contemplate and push myself upright. My head feels like it's going to explode with the movement as the pressure shifts radically.

"Who the fuck are you?" A sound that's something like a

groan and a curse escapes from the depths of hell. "And what the fuck happened?" How many ways can you use *fuck* in a sentence. Well, Alex, let me count the ways.

But it will have to wait until after I get the world to stop spinning. My stomach is none too happy about that fact.

"Well, you decided to cross the line between *hoah* and stupid, and picked a fight over the goddamned Army football team with a guy who works for one of the big mercenary companies. Turns out, he played for Navy and decided to take offense to your jokes."

"Oh, come on. It's not like everyone doesn't know Navy sucks their own—"

"Shut the fuck up, Caleb." How does this guy know my name? And who the hell does he think he is? "This has to stop."

I push up to my feet, using the cold brick wall behind me to keep myself standing. "I'm sorry but who the hell are you?"

"I'm your fairy fucking godfather."

The man in front of me looks like a cross between my eighth grade priest, Father Silvio and an extra from Orange County Choppers. He's sporting a red bandana, rolled up into a headband – a headband that's not really necessary considering the massive bald spot. The handlebar mustache makes him look like Hulk Hogan when he turned into one of the bad guys in the WWE. And I'm honestly not sure if the patches on his vest mean he's in a biker gang or just got a discount on cross stitch at Hobby Lobby. It's hard to tell these days. I mean, if I was a biker, I'd probably know but I'm not. I'm just some dude with a tattoo fetish and too much time on his hands to drink his liver into submission every night.

Father Biker really does look like a goddamned biker

priest. Which is a really weird combination when you think about it. Who the hell is saving souls on the back of a Harley Davidson? And sure enough, there's a Fatboy at the end of the alley. Because of course this nightmare includes a Harley. Why wouldn't it?

Time for this nightmare to end. I need to drag my ass home and sleep off the rest of this hangover. Army football is playing tonight and I don't want to miss the game because my liver is a fucking pussy.

"I don't need a fairy godfather. Or mother."

I look down at the black rose on my forearm, encased in thorns. I need to get the thorns finished. The brick scrapes my palms as I push off the wall.

"That's where you're wrong. See, at the end of this alley is a cop, waiting to take your happy ass to Durham County. Since I built a table for his wife for their twentieth anniversary, he's doing me a favor by not dragging your ass to jail."

"Why the hell do you care?"

"Because it's time for you to stop drinking yourself to death every night."

"You don't know anything about me."

"I know more than you think. I know why you drink. It's time to put away childish things."

His words are dark and laced with authority.

Turns out, I have a problem with authority. Ten miserable years in military school didn't break me of that.

"Hey, you know what?" I push off the wall again. The light from The Pint behind me spins wildly and black stars start to dance in front of my eyes. "How about you go fuck yourself, okay?"

"That's actually not anatomically possible, and it's oh so much more fun with a willing partner. But I wouldn't expect you to know that, whiskey dick."

I sway dangerously but I'm not backing down from this fucking guy. And if I can't beat Grandpa in a fight, well, then maybe it's time for me to turn in my man card. "I don't know if you think you're getting a blow job or a Good Samaritan award but I don't need or want your help."

I push off from the wall for the last time and start walking away from my wannabe savior, hoping I'm not as unsteady as I feel.

Until his words send a chill racing over my skin. Like a ghost has walked over my grave.

A ghost I know. A ghost of someone I miss more than life itself.

"Where are you going, Caleb?"

1

____

Two Months Later

Caleb

I used to think storms in Texas were bad. Then I moved to North Carolina and got exposed to a whole new world of violence, courtesy of Mother Nature. Of course, in Texas, I drove everywhere and I usually didn't find myself out in said storms.

I'm regretting my life choices, the ones that made me decide to stop driving everywhere when I decided to stop drinking. I only live a few blocks from Bruce's shop and a few blocks from the main strip in downtown Durham so I can easily walk everywhere. But it turns out, I should have started keeping track of the weather reports, especially when I'm out late working in Bruce's shop because, well, sleep is overrated.

Right now, his rule that no one sleeps with the power tools is a real pain in the balls. He closes the doors to his

Maker studio at midnight every night, right when my insomnia is just kicking into high gear. So tonight instead of sleeping, I decided on a fresh tattoo.

A reminder that I'm still lost somewhere on the road to Hell. And by that I mean sobriety.

I'm about two months late on step two of the keep-my-ass-sober plan.

Step One was *Stop drinking*. Step One B was not to kill anyone or myself while doing it.

Step Two is *Try to do normal things*. Because working for Bruce's contract company and building furniture on the side in his Maker Space—which is basically a glorified arts and crafts studio for men getting in touch with their crafty sides but with 3D printers and power tools, and I should just make a Tim the Toolman grunting noise at this point—and getting tattoos in the middle of the night are totally normal things for Army vets to do as ways of avoiding their PTSD, right?

It's taken me a really long fucking time to get to Step Two. And contrary to popular belief, getting a tattoo is something normal, especially for Army dudes. Maybe not officers but, well, I'm not an officer anymore. This tattoo is something that makes me feel like I'm still me. I'm still here.

It's been about six years since I got my first tattoo, during my first duty assignment at Fort Hood. I went all in on that one. It took six weekends in a row, flat on my stomach while I marked my back with the crucifix my mother used to wear. Then there was the tribal First Cav patch on my right shoulder. Then the rose twisted in a tangled briar down my left forearm.

I just need to figure out what normal is, without the alcohol.

I'm not entirely sure I'm going to actually make it to Step

Three, which involves finding a hobby and doing something that could marginally be called productive.

I don't know what that feels like anymore. Vega—the man in charge of making me look like a mental patient—takes one last swipe at my wrists, smears a thick coat of Aquaphor over them, and then wraps them in gauze. "Keep 'em covered for a day. Wash gently. Don't pick. Wrists are hard to heal because they're so bendy."

Two bandages. One on each wrist. Yep, I look like a fucking mental ward escapee.

And sadly, I know what that fucking feels like. I didn't count on the little white bandages setting off a cascade of really shitty memories.

My skin starts to crawl as I step out of the shade from the tattoo studio and right into an early morning storm. Fuck. I forgot about the weather rolling in.

I walk past The Pint, the bar where I've spent the better part of the last two years, since I arrived in Durham, trying to murder my liver.

It's time to go, Eli said.

And I knew that that was going to be the last time I set foot in the bar. He never told me I had to leave. Never told me I couldn't come back.

But somehow, being sober around him...it's too fucking hard. Because he *knows* things that everyone else doesn't and...I'm not ready to confront the reality of those things without being half in the bag.

So I've been avoiding The Pint. And Eli. And everyone else.

Because funny thing about being sober: you can remember all the horrible obnoxious shit you said when you were drunk and, well, it's really hard to own up to that.

I'll get there. Maybe.

I've gotten pretty good at burning all my bridges. All the guys I used to get hammered with are done now, peeled off and spending time with their significant others. Noah Warren was the first of our merry band of miscreants to get sober. Meeting Beth was what finally gave him the strength to try and get clean. Josh followed, though with a little less religious intensity than Noah. I'm pretty sure Abby is strong enough to keep Josh in line, though, and I was kind of a fucking asshole to her. She's fucking terrifying and competent and she would have made one hell of an officer if she'd ever decided to join the Army.

It sucks to wake up one day and realize that you're the drunk that no one wants to be around but they're too good to tell you that you suck. Not too many ways to earn your way back onto the island when your sobriety is questionable and...well, you get the idea.

The rain is coming down sideways in sheets. Violence fills the sky, threatening to send roofs and mobile homes, clinging to the edge of civilization outside of Durham, over the rainbow.

Tornado warnings in Texas always scared the shit out of me but at least I knew they were coming for miles—you could see them rolling in over the vast flat hill country.

Not here. Storms in North Carolina come out of nowhere and bring with them a pounding that the entire field artillery corps would be proud of.

Except that when you're caught out in this shit, you're not really thinking through how the concussion blast of a paladin would knock you off your ass. You really just want out of the damn rain that feels like razors on your skin.

'Course, I wouldn't have this problem if I hadn't decided to take the scenic route home. Past The Pint. Because I wanted to see if I could do it. If I could walk by and not feel the pull to walk in and ask Deacon to pour me a pint. To see if I could drink without being an asshole and drinking myself into oblivion. I thought I could handle it but the pull is still strong—still need twisted up with loss.

This month is going to be a shit month full of shitty personal anniversaries, but I forgot that it was also The Pint's five-year anniversary. At five a.m. the party is still going strong.

It takes everything I am to keep walking, to ignore how bad I want to step inside and feel happiness for my former friends.

The severe storm warning on my phone now includes hail. "Good times," I mutter, seriously considering if I can make it back to my apartment before all hell breaks loose outside—but I'm not really that brave.

I'm not brave at all, to be honest.

I've risked my life for less, but I'm really not looking to get knocked unconscious by a random ice ball so I need to find a place to ride out this monster storm. Even if my apartment is only about six blocks away, when the rain is slicing at your skin, six blocks might as well be six miles.

The only thing open is the yoga studio. I've walked past it a million times and never really paid attention to it until now, but I guess my options for getting out of the storm are pretty limited. What the hell kind of name is Arjuna for a yoga studio anyway? I thought they had to be named, like, Sacred Toadstool or some New Age shit. The sky explodes nearby and I try not to jump out of my fucking skin. "Fuck me."

My phone flashes a red warning: *Tornado and golf ball-size hail. Take shelter immediately.* Awesome.

I decide that the better part of bravery is to not be outside, or anywhere near a window when all hell breaks loose, and I duck into the yoga studio. I'd rather face the irritation of a stranger over Mother Nature's fury any day of the week.

Inside, there's an immediate flash of warmth combined with a scent of something spicy and equally warm from incense burning in a corner. A hint of *something* lies just at the edge of my memory—something familiar and just *there*...and then it's gone.

I'm pretty sure my ass is going to end up spending the rest of the day in a goddamned basement, the way my phone continues to wail with new emergency notifications like it's the goddamned Apocalypse outside.

That could be about as much fun as getting shot. Which is not nearly as bad as it sounds. It's the rehab that's a motherfucker, or so I hear.

The woman behind the counter looks up as the door closes behind me. The sound of chimes rings out from the studio behind her. Her expression tells me I must look like a fucking crisis actor, soaking wet, like something the cat dragged in.

She's vaguely familiar but I can't place where I know her from. Her jet-black hair is pulled back in a loose knot at the base of her neck and her skin is a warm, deep copper, the color of sand on a beach at dusk. Her eyes grab me—soft, brown, and deeply intense. She moves with a smooth precision that makes me think *this woman knows her place in this life.*

I watch her physically straighten as her gaze drifts down soaking wet me. I wonder if she sees what I do when I look in the mirror. Does she notice the cuts on my hands from Bruce's tools or the dark circles under my eyes?

I breathe in deeply, trying to grasp hold of the familiar sensation dancing at the edge of my mind. But it slips away again, leaving me alone. But at least that sensation is familiar.

She can't see me. No one can, not if they're not close enough. I've made sure of that.

Her gaze lands back on my face and she inhales deeply, as if she's bracing for conflict.

I'm suddenly not sure if I'd rather be facing the storm outside, or if there is one right in front of me.

Maybe she's afraid. Maybe she knows who I am. Maybe being around me is *toxic*. The word is bitter in my chest.

Maybe I deserve that reaction. I haven't exactly been Prince Charming for the last few years. The realization is still hard to accept and even harder to try and change and, well...maybe I should try to get out of the habit of lying to myself these days.

I don't know how to do this. How to have a normal conversation with someone. I don't know what I'm doing here except that I wanted to get out of the storm.

I can't remember the last time I had a conversation with a woman where I wasn't loaded to the gills.

I suppose there's no time like the present and all that, right?

"Can I help you?" She's stiff but trying not to be. I recognize the signs now, of someone who doesn't want to be where they are. I guess that's Bruce's influence.

Is that good? That I can see when someone is uncomfortable? Even if the source of that discomfort is me and only me?

What the fuck am I supposed to do with the knowledge?

I open my mouth, hoping to say something that isn't

completely appalling. Hoping to say something normal like, *Hi, I was just trying to get out of the storm. Great shop.*

Instead, I stand there, my lips parted but no sound coming out.

Mute. Knowing she's nervous. Knowing I'm cold.

Knowing there is nothing I can do to bridge the gap between us. Because someone like her will always be afraid of me.

And maybe she should be.

~

Nalini

"HOLY SHIT!" The explosion sounds like lightning's struck the ground somewhere close outside. It vibrates through my chest, ripping the air from my lungs. My heart slams against my ribs, my scream tears blood and tissue on its way out of my throat.

Seeing how he ducks at the sound of the blast, too, I'm at least not worried about salvaging my pride. That fear and the look in his eyes make him seem like less of a threat. I'm oddly relieved that I'm *probably* not about to be robbed at gunpoint by the soaking wet meth addict standing in the doorway of my studio.

Maybe he just looks a little strung out from insomnia. That's what I'm going to tell myself, anyway.

Behind the shadows in his eyes there is something compelling, something that's drawn me to him from the moment he stepped inside my studio. Even as the rational part of my brain was tempted to press the panic button.

Then I'm blinded by an alarm flashing from the cell phone on my desk. "You're welcome to join me in the basement or not but you have to get away from the glass," I tell him quickly.

He frowns. "I'm sorry?"

"Tornado warning. Isn't that why you ducked in here?"

Awareness fills his eyes and he nods. "Um, yeah."

I can't tell if he's drunk or high. And while spending the morning hanging out in the basement with a complete stranger when I'm supposed to be teaching my first yoga class isn't exactly a great way to start a week, clearly the universe has other plans for me.

I move quickly as the sky fills with light again, flicking the lock on the front door and motioning for him to follow me. The lights flicker from the studio above as we descend the stairs and I offer a quick prayer that they'll stay on.

I hate basements. There's something primordial and terrifying about descending into the literal bowels of the earth, especially now, with hell raging in the sky overhead. As we step into the basement, the studio goes dark as the power finally surrenders to the storm. The flashlight on my phone pierces the darkness and chases away any demons that might be living among my yoga mats and extra stock.

But that light won't last forever. And I need to find a candle before the battery runs out.

Of course, I'm using the space for storage. I'd be a fool not to. I just usually ask Cricket—my office manager, who is not afraid of anything—to supervise the retrieval of things from the dark.

I fumble for the basement light switch at the bottom and my hand collides with another warm hand. "Jesus!"

"Sorry."

The fact that it's the wet guy's hand and not attached to an evil spirit in the dark makes me ridiculously happy. I reach out, touching flesh that is warm and solid and male.

Of course, then the power goes out completely and we are plunged into near complete darkness, with the only light coming from my cell phone. "Almost forgot you'd followed me." There's no hiding the panic in my voice. I hate the dark.

"I'm so fucking glad you're not a zombie." His voice is dry and droll. So completely at odds with everything I'm feeling. The laugh steals out of me. I can't help it. It's better than crying. The panic of stepping into the dark isn't gone, but the laugh helps. I don't take my fingers from his. I'm terrified and panicked enough to need the human connection right now.

I hate the dark. No matter how much I meditate, the chasm that opened inside me on my deployment to Syria—the deployment that didn't officially exist—hasn't closed.

"The feeling is entirely mutual," I finally manage.

I am intensely aware of the heat from his skin penetrating his damn T-shirt. The solid warmth and the steady rhythm of his pulse beneath my fingers.

He moves then, and his palm covers the back of my hand. "Are you okay?"

That is such an infinitely loaded question with a thousand ways to answer.

"Not really." It's so easy to admit the vulnerability to a stranger. Here in the dark with the violence raging overhead. "I don't like storms."

"Me either. Haven't really enjoyed them since Iraq."

My fingers flex against this stranger's skin, reaching toward the common bond I didn't realize we shared. "Army?"

"Yes." He captures my hand. "You're freezing."

"So are you." He shivers as the words brush over my skin. "Did you know panic tends to use your blood for other things? Appendages staying warm isn't a priority when you're running for your life." I slip my hand from his, stepping into the darkness to the rack where my yoga blankets are stacked neatly. "Here." I toss him a black and white and red wool blanket.

"Damn, this is softer than it looks." He slings it around his shoulders. "Thank you. Would it be unmanly of me to admit I'm freezing my balls off?"

I wrap up in a blanket, too, and step closer to him. Because I don't want to be alone in the dark.

"If the dark fucks you up, why not have backup power or something?" he asks when I don't answer.

Such a pragmatic suggestion, but utterly useless when I've got all I can handle just avoiding triggers when the lights are on. "Guess you didn't hear that part about the panic?"

I toss a couple of meditation pillows onto the floor.

"Can we use this?" He lifts a fat white candle off a shelf.

"Yeah. Not sure how long the storm will last."

He sets it down and I try not to notice the way his body moves. He's not graceful. He's...rough. Stiff. As though life has already been incredibly hard on his body. "Do you have anything to light this with?"

"I think so." I vaguely recall something about ceremonial matches that Cricket had stored down here and the moment I find them I love her more than I already did.

He slips the matches from my hand and lights the squat fat candle. He doesn't demand to know why I didn't light it myself. Doesn't question the shaking of my hands that I hide by clicking off my cell phone light as soon as the candle flame lights up the darkness.

I sit on one of the meditation cushions, folding my legs in front of me, far enough away from the candle that I can't feel its warmth, but close enough that I'm within the circle of light spread by its tiny flame.

The edge of his mouth curls a little. He's still watching me, those dark eyes filled with...something I can't identify.

Something I'm afraid to acknowledge. Something tainted with fear.

"I'm Caleb," he says after a moment.

The air in the basement is cold. My bones ache now when I get cold. That's new since coming home from the war. I try to ignore it. But sometimes it rears up and reminds me that I still hurt.

Like now. In this moment, the simple human connection of telling someone my name is a needed distraction from the memories raging with the storm outside. "I'm Nalini."

He's focused and intense, like rubbing my freezing fingers is the most important thing in the world. "I went to school with a Nalini once upon a time."

"It was my grandmother's name."

"It's Hindi, isn't it?"

It's funny how a benign conversation can draw you away from the edge of panic. "Yeah. Most people don't know that."

"I'm not most people."

I smile faintly. "Apparently."

He sits next to me, soaking wet and wrapped in a yoga blanket. The shadows from the candlelight have cut his features, sharpening some, softening others. He's taller than I am, broader. He's a big man with a wide chest and strong hands.

I notice men's hands now. I notice whether they're manicured or rough. Whether the nails have been trimmed or broken.

Caleb's hands are rough. There's a fresh cut along the tops of his knuckles on one hand and each of his wrists are wrapped in bandages. I'm hoping those are from tattoos instead of something else.

I flinch as another explosion makes the walls around us shudder. Out of the corner of my eye, I notice he does the same. Despite the layers of building between us and Mother Nature's fury, the storm sounds like it's right on top of us. Maybe it is.

"Fuck, this is a bad one," he mutters.

"Yeah." The fear is back in my voice, shaking and violent. I need to focus. To try and find a way out of the narrow tunnel drawing me back to a violent hyper awareness I've tried to leave behind.

A siren blares in the darkness. He glances down at his phone. "Shelter in place," he reads, looking up at me. "I think we're going to be here a while." He shivers again.

"Do you want another blanket? I have sweatshirts in one of these boxes if you'd like to change." *Focus on the things I can control. Release the things I can't.*

Taking care of others is so much easier than taking care of myself.

"I'll manage." He sets the phone by his feet. "Thank you, though."

Any other time, being in the dark like this would erode the fragile remains of my soul that I've pieced back together over the last few years. But in that moment, the darkness isn't terrifying. Even the candle's flame, which I would normally hate, offers a golden-hued comfort. I am so grateful not to be in the dark, with the explosions and violence, alone.

I've been there before.

I keep trying not to go back. And every time I think I'm okay, that I've finally released the last of the terror and fear from the memory of my muscles and tissue and bones, it resurfaces.

Like now. With the storm tearing at the world overhead, my brain is trying desperately to remind my body that we are not in Syria, that we are not trapped.

That I am not burning.

2

———

Caleb

I adjust the cushion and lean back against the wall. What I really want to do is light a dozen more candles and get a small bonfire going but that wouldn't be very considerate of my host and products I'm confident she's trying to sell.

"How long do you think we'll be down here?" she asks after a long silence.

It's hard to miss the nervous edge in her voice. She's trying to hide it but it's far too obvious. She's watching the candle like a mouse watches a cat.

She's not doing too hot right now. To be honest, neither am I.

"I don't know?" I try to keep my voice from chattering from the cold. That's me, trying to be all manly and stoic, when I'm really just damn glad that I'm not alone riding this one out.

"The last I heard, it stretched from here to Alabama with

another round coming in over the Atlantic. Something about a double hurricane system."

"So we're caught in the middle. Awesome." I sigh and try not to shiver too obviously.

She makes a noise. "I should have grabbed my cell phone charger." There is blame in her voice, like she's punishing herself for leaving it behind.

"Not sure how that helps with the power being out." I breathe out slowly. "At least we've got the candle."

"Until we don't." She shifts, leaning back on the wall next to me. I try not to notice the warmth radiating from her body. "So, Caleb. What were you doing out in a five-in-the-morning storm?"

I glance over at her. "Working off my insomnia."

Her faint smile fades, her eyes filling with an insidious fear I recognize all too well. "And how were you doing that, that you got caught in the storm?"

"I was building a table at my boss's Maker warehouse. When he closed it down at midnight, I decided to hang out downtown rather than head home. And since I'm a dumbass who didn't check the weather, here I am."

Ignoring the fear underlying her questions is the polite thing to do. It's something Bruce taught me. Something I'm working on. Learning to read other people's emotions through what they don't say. Sometimes, saying nothing is the right thing. No one likes to have their panic and fear used against them.

"If you weren't doing this right now, how would you have spent this morning?" I'm curious. "I'm not sure I've ever been in a yoga studio before."

"I'm not sure I've ever met anyone who wasn't sure if they'd been to a yoga studio before." She cups her head in her hand, bracing her elbow on her knee. "I'd be teaching a morning Iyengar yoga level two class."

"So...like twisting people into pretzels and shit?"

Her lips twitch at the corners. "Your knowledge of yoga is just good enough to be entirely wrong." But there is no malice in her voice. She frowns at me and gives me what I can only assume is a wicked side eye. "The asana practice involves moving meditation. It's only one of the eight limbs of yoga."

"Eight limbs? Who knew? I thought it was all yoga pants and vegan hippies."

I'm teasing her, trying to take her mind off the fear I see skirting in the shadows around her eyes. I might be dead ass tired but I'm also keenly aware that I'm a strange man that she doesn't know and she's well within her rights to be wary. If I can put her at ease...well, that maybe makes me a little bit less of an asshole.

And these days, every little bit counts.

"Not even close." She rubs her index finger down the center of her forehead. She is stillness in that movement. It's fascinating. "I could talk all morning about the problems with yoga in the West but that would probably put you at risk of running back into the storm."

It's my turn to tip my head and look at her. "Why do you say that?"

"Most folks eye roll pretty hard when problematic culture is identified."

I nod slowly. I'm afraid to ask what she's talking about, afraid to ruin the hesitant peace between us by asking the wrong question.

She shifts and I can't miss how she pulls her legs away from the flame. "You don't like the dark but you don't like candles either?"

"It's a long war story with lots of personal trauma," she says in the dry way that only a veteran can. The biting edge of black humor that only someone who has stared into the abyss of war can understand.

"I'll tell you mine if you tell me yours."

That makes her smile. Just barely; it cracks the edges of her lips. She threads her fingers into her hair and rests an elbow against her bent knee. "Sure. I mean, if you can't confess your darkest personal trauma to a complete stranger while hiding from a force *majeure*, who can you tell?"

I glance away, toward the tiny candle. It's amazing how the small source of light illuminates so much. "So. What does a five a.m. yoga class involve?"

"Five thirty. Slow movements, building tapas—energy—for the day. Rituals that facilitate awakening."

I mirror her posture, resting my forehead against my palm. "Why so early?"

"Lots of demand for the specific type of yoga I offer, I guess."

"Wait; there are different types of yoga?"

She stretches one leg out in front of her—away from the flame—and bends forward, until her cheek hovers just above her knee. "Yes. There are lots of different styles. Asana is just one piece. Some are more ancient than others. It's a philosophy, a way of life."

"I'm thoroughly confused," I confess. "What's *asana*?"

"Sorry. It's the movement portion of yoga. The poses."

Her breathing is deep and rhythmic as she straightens and bends over the other leg.

"The breathing limb of yoga is *pranayama*."

"And is there something specific that you're doing now?" I find the sound of her breathing, like the sound of the wind in a conch shell, enthralling.

Finally, she offers a faint smile. "This particular pose is called 'attempting not to panic-asana'," she says with a lightness that does not match her words.

"Panic seems like a pretty distinct emotion." I'm afraid to ask more but I'm also curious now. Here's a woman who is running her own yoga studio, who clearly deployed to the Middle East, slinging around the word "panic" as if she's talking about something completely different, like...how much she loves a particular kind of chocolate.

I sit with her in the faint light of the candle, listening to her just breathe. Feeling the stillness.

Embraced in a cocoon of darkness and light, safe from the storm raging outside.

Nalini

*J*UST BREATHE.

The squat fat candle is bravely pushing back the darkness around us. A single flame, gallantly holding back the wave of crushing fear that lurks at the edge of the shadows.

Those candles have never sold particularly well. It's hard to market a candle like this one—ungainly, with one wick—when people seem convinced that only expensive, heavily scented glass candles are the only ones of value.

At the moment, though, I'm grateful for the whole damn box of them, even if I would never burn them all at once. That'd be far too much fire in one place.

"Why?"

I glance over at him and it takes me a moment to realize I've spoken out loud about the fire. *Shit.*

"Why what?"

"Why are you afraid of the fire?"

I chew on the inside of my lip, debating how far I should take this conversation. Part of me thinks of him as a single-serving friend from Flight Club—that person you sit with on a plane and share your deepest fears and secrets with, only to never see them again.

But another part of me, the part of me that's drawn to the warmth of his skin radiating against mine, the part of me that is seriously grateful for his kindness in getting the candle going without pushing for too many answers to unasked questions...that part of me is more leery.

For a guy who wandered in off the street looking like a half-drowned stray, my storm buddy is turning into quite an interesting puzzle.

"Bad memories of my mom's cooking as a kid." I make a feeble attempt at a joke. The candle flickers and struggles to stay lit.

"Oh." There is so much disappointment in that single syllable, as if I've lost an opportunity that I'll never have again.

I need to change the subject, away from my paralyzing, irrational panic to something more mundane. Instead, I decide to embrace it, to name the thing that makes me afraid. "I was trapped in a building in Syria. I've had some...issues with fire since then. So not being in the dark alone makes this whole thing a lot easier."

"Is it the storm or the darkness?" Every time he speaks, his voice vibrates through the connection of our arms. His voice is deep and rough. Like the darkness in his eyes.

"Both? I think it's the combination that makes it tougher than normal."

Silence hangs between us, heavy, then filled with the sounds of the battle in the sky overhead. It sounds as if the lightning is striking the ground all around the studio, and even through the closed doors and layers of concrete, we can hear the wind howling like a mad thing, clawing at the earth as if it would drag us from safety.

"I used to sit with my mother and listen to the thunderstorms when I was a kid," he says after a moment.

"Yeah?"

"Yeah. When we lived at Fort Hood. Our house was out on Stillhouse Hollow, overlooking the water. We could watch the storms roll across the hill country through these huge glass windows. Storms always remind me of how she used to smell. Like no matter where I am, I can always smell the lotion she used to wear." He clears his throat. "Crabtree and Evelyn Rosewater. Even in Iraq, I could still remember the way she smelled."

"You're talking in past tense." I'm afraid to speak the words. To ask the question his words imply.

"She died when I was twelve." I feel him tense, a physical manifestation of the pain of a lost boy in those simple words. "She was killed the first year we were in Iraq. One of the first women to die in our endlessly stupid war."

His words slam into me, a solid punch in the chest, crushing my heart into a thousand shining pieces. I reach for him in the dark, finding his hand resting on his thigh. He doesn't resist as I thread my fingers in his. "I'm sorry."

"She's why I joined the Army." He lifts his hand, breaking the contact between us, scrubbing it over his face. "Sorry. I haven't been sleeping well. Didn't mean to dump that on you."

I don't remove my hand from where it rests on his thigh. "It's okay."

He makes a noise, his hand covering his eyes. "I never

really talk about her. I think you're the first person I've told in...forever."

"A loss like that would tend to be hard to talk about." The muscle in his leg is knotted and tense, his words strained. Like the words are dragging the physical pain back out from a place he does not want to go.

"I got lucky. The first person I told was one of my roommates at school. I never told anyone except him. He never fucked with me about it. Never called me a baby for tearing up."

"What kind of a bastard would tease anyone for being sad about their mom dying?"

"Clearly, you don't know cadets," he says dryly.

I stiffen at his words. The possibility of him being a member of the Long Gray Line like me is...unsettling, at best.

I've tried my hardest to avoid fellow West Pointers as a rule. I do not have good memories of that place. No matter how much it set me up for success, the price I paid...I can't say it was worth it. "West Point?"

"Yep. Class of 2012."

"Small world. I'm class of 2010." I angle my shoulders slightly toward him.

He shifts then, peering over at me. "No shit? Why haven't you ever been over to The Pint? I thought Eli had rounded up all the local veterans and Old Grads."

I want to avoid the subject of the veteran community in Durham. There are good folks here—my issues are mine, not theirs. "I've been too busy building my business. Yoga is a highly competitive marketplace and I'm trying to establish a foothold in an already crowded city."

"Really? There's that many people that want to get together with a bunch of people and chant?"

I'm used to people knowing very little about yoga or the philosophy and beliefs behind it. Misconceptions are not offensive to me unless they're intentional or exploitative. Don't get me started on the exploitation. So I don't correct him, not right then. As much as yoga is fundamental to who I am, I'm not offended by his lack of knowledge or the flippant way he talks about it.

He doesn't know any different and for some reason, I have an extraordinary amount of patience for my storm buddy. That doesn't make his comments any less problematic. It just means I'm less likely to argue about it today.

"You should drop by The Pint sometime. Eli...well, never mind. I'm kind of on a self-imposed ban at the moment."

I'm uncomfortably aware of my hand on his thigh, the solid strength beneath my touch. He lowers his then, and sets it on mine.

It's an easy thing to flip mine beneath his so we're palm to palm. An intimately human connection between two strangers.

Funny how that works. Stripped away of everything, all pretense, all the noise of modern life, we can sit here and be fully human, fully aware of everything we are to each other. Absorbing each other's energy.

"Why are you self-imposing a ban?"

His fingers flex beneath mine. "I'm coming off a ten-year run of being a complete fucking asshole."

3

Caleb

She says nothing for a long time. The storm thrashes above us, its violence reminding me far too closely of the sounds of mortar and rocket attacks on our tiny base in northern Iraq. It's showing no sign of letting up, even after almost an hour. I'm not used to storms hanging around like this. The storms in the hill country usually rolled through pretty quickly.

I don't hate storms. I wasn't lying when I told her they made me think of my mother. They do. But those memories are twisted up now, and tied into the explosions and bullshit from Iraq.

So it's complicated. Just like everything in my life.

One thing that hasn't gotten too terribly complicated at this moment is being with the woman next to me, even though I'm still curious about why she's afraid of the dark. I know there's more there.

Sitting there, listening to the crashing storm, it's far too easy to confess the harsh reality of my own life that I haven't really unpacked for anyone.

Ever.

Eli knows part of it. Hell, he knows most of it. That's a big part of the reason he put up with me for so damn long.

Deacon got sick of pretending to care.

Noah and Josh walked away a long time ago.

I'm sorry. I've managed to run off everyone who was ever decent to me. I'll run you off, too, I think. But I say none of those things.

"I thought you were friends with Eli."

"I was. I am." I love the feeling of her palm pressed to mine. The simple connection of skin to skin. "He's...a good friend. The roommate I told about my mom? That was Eli. He was such a Boy Scout, even then." I don't mean that disparagingly. Eli is one of the best men I know.

It's then that I notice the copper design tracing down the back of her index finger. "What's this?"

She slips her hand from mine and holds both of hers out in front of her. "Henna. I came home from one of my cousins' weddings in Mumbai last week."

I reach for her before I realize it might be rude. She smiles and there's a light in her eyes that wasn't there a moment ago. "It's okay. It's part of the *mehndi* ceremony. The bride's arms, hands, and legs are decorated with powerful protective symbols using henna. Tradition says that the darker her henna is and the longer it lasts predicts how much her husband will love her."

"That's so neat." I trace my finger over the looping flowers and swirls, then turn her hand over, noticing the designs that are more faded on her palms. "Does it hurt?"

I glance up and see her noticing the scrapes on my fingers, the black tattoos peeking out from the edges of my sleeves. She meets my gaze but doesn't ask the question I see in her eyes.

"No," she tells me. "It's applied as a paste. It dries and flakes off and continues to darken for the next day or so. It actually cools as it dries."

"It's beautiful." The silence draws out between us again. "So before Syria, did you always hate storms?" I ask, needing to fill the space with something other than the noise of the destruction above us.

"They're calling this a hundred years' storm," she says. "At this point, I'm hoping the building doesn't get destroyed so I don't have to cancel classes."

"That's not answering the question." I slide my thumb over the designs on her skin. The touch is gentle. I'm seeking rather than taking. Unsure of how long she will allow this contact to remain. I'll enjoy the connection for however long it lasts. Because pure human contact has been in short supply in my life for so goddamned long.

And it will end. Of that, I'm certain. It always does.

"No, I didn't always hate storms," she says after a moment. "West Point started me on the path of astraphobia and getting blown up in Syria sealed the deal."

"You know it's treatable, right?"

"So is smoking, drinking, and sex addiction. Doesn't mean I'm going to let someone pick through my head when it's perfectly reasonable to be afraid of something that can kill you." She removes her hand from mine, dragging her fingers through her hair. Her breathing is coming faster, harder.

As if she catches my thoughts, she slows it down. Deeply inhaling, then controlling the exhale. It's impressive watching her reclaim control.

"We can talk about something else," I say. "Childhood pets. Pet peeves. Favorite stupid new cadet story."

She closes her eyes, resting her head against the concrete wall behind us. "On my summer detail as a yearling, one of my new cadets swallowed a live grasshopper during Beast because one of the cadre NCOs dared her to."

God, but it feels so weird to talk about yearlings and plebes and cows and not have to explain that Beast is essentially basic training. Plebes are freshmen and basically pond scum. We'd talk about them like they were houseplants or pets. They didn't even have names until they made it through freshman year. Yearlings or yuks are sophomores, cows are juniors and firsties—first class cadets are seniors. It's so damn strange to fall right back into the language of West Point, even though it's been years since I graduated.

It's really hard to laugh when you're both amused yet horrified, and I somehow manage to be both at the same time. "What the hell? Why would anyone do that?"

"Which part? The swallowing of the live bug or the daring someone to swallow said live bug?"

"Both? Either. Hell, I thought I'd seen everything." I shudder at the idea of a living thing's feet prickling down my throat on its way to an acid bath. Ugh.

"Clearly you've never wanted to belong so badly to something that you'd do anything for acceptance."

Her words strike a nerve. One she doesn't realize is exposed. I rest my elbow on one knee, pushing my hair back. It's too long now. Kind of like the scruff on my face that's rapidly passed the stage of five o'clock shadow and is moving into full beard mode. I need to shave before I start blending in with all the hippies around here. "You have no idea."

She presses her lips into a flat line. "I'm sorry."

"Why?"

"It seems like I keep circling back and saying things that aren't really...they're pretty insensitive."

"I've had a long time to get over losing my mom." The words are forced bravado, pushing back against the knot that rises up against my throat. A lie, convenient and dark, blending into the shadows.

"No one gets over that. No matter how old they are." She shifts, moving her body into contact with mine once more. A living, breathing being pressed against another living being, unsure of how to offer comfort except through contact.

"How do you know to do that?" I ask suddenly.

"Do what?"

"You just...you keep pressing against me."

She moves away. "Sorry. Didn't mean to..."

I slip my hand around her knee, holding her fast. "I didn't mean it like it sounded." I release her quickly. "It's just...not something people do all the time. I noticed, that's all."

The candlelight flickers over her, casting her honey gold skin in even deeper copper hues. Her full lips are parted, dark and dusky and fucking erotic as hell. If I close my eyes, my brain will definitely go someplace not appropriate for polite company.

"Our bodies and minds are connected. Seventy percent of human communication is nonverbal." Her voice is quiet beneath the storm. "Sometimes, it's easier to express something without saying a word."

"That's...fascinating." I'm practicing not being an asshole. Or rather, practicing directness without being an asshole. Once upon a time, I would have called what she's said hippy New Age bullshit.

Amazing how sobriety can change your point of view on oh...everything.

"I'm glad." Her words are a comfort. A balm I hadn't realized I needed.

"I'm glad I'm not alone right now."

Nalini

MY BREATH CATCHES in my throat. His words are a caress. A teasing promise of something deeper than a brush of skin against skin in the dark.

But also a connection, something deeply human that binds us together. It's not just our shared fear of the dark. It's something...different. Deeper.

More human.

"The universe has a strange way of making things happen that need to happen," I say after a drawn-out silence.

His arm flexes as he drags his hand through his hair once more. "I'm not sure I believe that."

Too late, I realize my words have sliced at him without meaning to. I reach for him then because I can do nothing else but apply pressure to the wound I've opened, no matter how unintentionally. I didn't mean to, but I guess knowing about his mother's death has turned into something I can't avoid, even if I'm trying to. "I'm sorry. I know how callous it must sound for someone to say everything happens for a reason."

He doesn't pull away. "But that's not what you were saying. Was it?"

"It wasn't. But I can see how it might have sounded like

that." I glance over at him—the shadow of scruff on his jaw, his deep eyes. The lure of him that much stronger. I've never felt this before. This connection to someone I've known for an hour at best. This strong compulsion for *more*. "I think the hardest thing for humans to do is to explain suffering and pain. Why does it exist? Why can't we make it go away? It's not possible to imagine a world without suffering and pain."

"Is that how you choose to deal with it? By believing everything has a purpose?" His words are measured. Controlled. Constricted in a way they hadn't been a few moments earlier.

I lean away from him a bit, resting my elbows on my knees and pushing my hair out of my face, twisting it into a thick bun on the top of my head.

"I don't know. For me, it's less about whether or not there's some God up there controlling the world and more about...just trying to believe that I'm where I need to be."

"Even when shit sucks in an unforgettable way?"

"Especially then," I whisper. I can't tell him about the fire. About the burning, clawing panic that tore away my sense of self that I'd worked so hard to build. Or the struggle to put my life back together after I finally realized I wasn't going to die if I suddenly had a hard time breathing.

He shifts next to me, straightening one leg out in front of him. "I wish I could look at life like that."

"It took me a really long time. In a lot of ways, I'm still struggling with it." I've got a handle on things now. I can sit near fire and not freak out. But the work to get here...yeah, it's been one hell of a journey.

His throat moves as he swallows. "Yeah? How?"

"Well, for instance, there was an incident the other

morning. I may have reacted a little strongly when I walked into the barbecue joint that's opening next door."

One side of his gorgeous full bottom lip lifts upward. "Oh, do tell."

"I may have threatened the owner with neutering." I flush. I'll blame the wicked sensuality of that upturned lip instead of my own embarrassment over the incident. "We could call what happened a strong disagreement."

"Honey, neutering isn't a strong disagreement. Those would be fighting words for most men."

Funny how him calling me "honey" in that moment doesn't scrape against my skin. There's something about his smile, hidden in the shadows, that warms the space around my heart. He has a really great smile. Like it surprises *him* every time it happens. There's a shyness to him, an uncertainty buried in the quiet strength of this man.

He's staring at me and I am unable to look away from the shadows lingering in his eyes, always there. Ever present. Brooding. I've never really thought about what a brooding man looks like in real life but I think I've finally seen it.

And now I understand why people find brooding compelling. Attractive.

I lick my lips, my mouth suddenly dry. His gaze darts to my lips, then back up again. I didn't think it was possible but his eyes have darkened now.

"Some things are worth fighting over," I finally whisper.

"Like not smelling barbecue when you're doing yoga?"

I return his smile then. Faintly, because it's dancing too close to my own scars—mental and physical. "Yeah. It's really unsettling for some people."

"By 'some people' do you mean you?"

I look away then, unable to find the words to tell him

about the war and the marks it left on me. "Sure. If that makes me seem less crazy."

I focus on the candle. The small, controlled flame that gives light in the eerie, cold cellar is the stuff of nightmares. It doesn't frighten me. It doesn't spark terrible nightmares. But a sense of something familiar washes over me, like I've done this before.

Funny how something so small and fragile can build into something capable of destroying the world with the right fuel.

He shifts before I can respond, his palm sliding over my knee to squeeze gently. "You don't have to tell me," he says softly. "Some things aren't easy to talk about."

I look away from the candle at the man sitting next to me. He's close. Closer than he should be. The heat from his body wraps around me, his scent an enthralling mixture of smoke and man. A good kind of mixture.

The kind that makes a girl want to do stupid things. Like crawl into his lap and cup his face. Rock gently against him while he kisses me slow and deep.

He catches me staring. And he doesn't look away. He's caught, just like me. Drawn into a shared need for warm human contact encased in the cold brick tomb that surrounds us. The quiet gasps of our bodies mixing with the violence from the storm overhead.

It's just a fantasy.

One I don't want to end.

4

Caleb

Being sober isn't all it's cracked up to be. There's arousal and awkward tension tightening in my belly, my heart pounding far too loudly in my head. I swallow hard, unwilling and unable to look away from the depths of her dark eyes. Eyes that make me feel like she can see into the recesses of my soul, to the nightmares that I've worked so hard to keep from showing the world.

It's a terrible thing, this sober desire. I wish I had the confidence I used to have when I was drunk, that I could reach for her and cup her face and savor the soft feel of her skin beneath my palm. That maybe she'd lean a little closer and I could nibble on her bottom lip like I was some kind of gracious lover, skilled at seducing women with a few whispered words and the stroke of my skin against theirs.

I've never done this before.

Her lips curl ever so slightly at the edges. "Done what, taken shelter with a stranger?"

I'm jolted by the awareness that I've said those words out

loud. I swallow again, hoping I can somehow salvage the terrible revelation. "That, too."

"Well, what did you mean if you didn't mean this?" Her voice is husky, as though she knows the secrets I don't want to tell.

"Been around a woman…" *Holy shit this is hard.* "That…ah…I find attractive, while sober."

I was better at it when I was hard drinking every night at The Pint. Or maybe I wasn't but I was too drunk to pick up on the social cues of the women around me.

Something flickers in her eyes but it's not the thing I fear. There's no judgment there. It's something else. Something I can't place.

"Thank you," she says softly.

It's my turn to be confused. "For what?"

"Sharing that. It's never easy to put the things that make us vulnerable out into the world."

I take in a deep breath, then release it, slowly. Deliberately. "Yeah, well, I'm working on that. Among other things."

"Yeah? What else?"

I shake my head, smiling slightly. "Nah, it's your turn. What's hard for you?" I'm not going to think it. Not going to think it…and I thought it. Damn it, I'm making inappropriate jokes in my head.

"Being with people."

I narrow my eyes. "You own a yoga studio. By definition that involves being with people."

She lifts one shoulder, then drops it slightly. "It's not the same. When I'm teaching a class or working with a client, it's different. There's a connection. A link. It's…it's hard to explain. But when I'm not teaching… Sometimes it's hard to find things to talk about. I have some pretty heavy duty nerd tendencies and I can keep talking long after your eyes have glazed over."

I'm starting to develop a thing for nerdy yogis with erotic brown eyes. This is the single most intriguing conversation I've had in a long time. Like, I can't remember the last time I just sat with someone and just...talked. "Tell me about your studio."

Granted, the storm overhead is a convenient forcing function.

I never thought I'd be grateful for the violent actions of Mother Nature.

"Well, my yoga studio is called Arjuna Yoga. Arjun is the warrior in the *Bhagavad Gita* who dialogues with Lord Krishna. I'm fascinated by Arjun's dialogue about violence. About war and how Krishna argued that it was Arjun's duty to fight. I started my studio because I...was having a hard time coming home after my deployment. I couldn't make sense of what we'd done or why we'd done it. So I went back to the stories my aunties told me as a child. And when I read the *Gita* again, something clicked for me." She stops herself, as though she's rushing and suddenly realizes it. "See. Told you. I'm a nerd. And I recognize that not everyone wants to have those kinds of conversations."

It's fascinating to listen to her. To watch her eyes flash with light as she talks. "I could listen to you talk about that all day," I say after a moment because I realize that I haven't said anything and the silence could get really awkward. "Aunties? How many aunts do you have?"

"I have five aunts and twelve great aunts on my mother's side and two aunts on my father's side."

I cough at the number, trying not to be incredibly rude. "What? How big is your family?"

"I'm half-Indian. My mother has two sisters and three

brothers. My father's family is much smaller. He only has two brothers."

"Wow. How can you have issues with people with a family that big?"

She smiles warmly. "It's different in India. Everyone is connected. Here, every connection takes more energy and some people are draining. It's not like that there. I can't describe it. It's like everyone knows you and you know everyone and people have known each other their entire lives. It's not like that here. At all."

"So wait. You're half-Indian but you went to West Point and deployed to Syria and now you're opening a yoga studio?" I lean back against the wall, slightly intimidated by everything she's accomplished. "How did you decide to go to West Point?"

She smiles. "I wanted to serve the country that gave my mother a home. I grew up hearing about my great grandfathers fighting in World War II. Britain depended on Indian fighters." She sighs. "And my great grandfathers came home from World War II and helped India win its independence from Britain."

I make a noise. "I had no idea about that part of British history."

"It's Indian history," she says and I feel like I've been gently corrected.

I make a note. "So that lead you to West Point?"

"Yeah. I mean, I wanted to serve. My great grandfathers all served. My father's grandmother was a hello girl in France. Serving seemed like the right thing to do."

I shift and rest my elbow against my knee. "That has got to be the most unique how I got to West Point story I've ever heard. You've had a seriously interesting life."

"Well, I didn't include the year I studied in India at the

Ramamanani Institute. Guru Iyengar named it after his wife." I love the way her gaze softens when she talks about India. The way her face lights up.

"This is fascinating." I've never met anyone who has spent time in India, let alone is from there. I have so many questions but I don't want to play the ignorant American. Well, at least not any more than I am already.

"That's me. Interesting life story that nobody is ever really interested in."

I tip my head. "Now I'm confused."

"Never mind. Let's just say that the farther I moved away from my family and my home, the more disconnected I felt. Yoga gives me a way to feel at home without having to hop on a twenty-hour flight to Mumbai."

"It's clearly something that matters to you." I clear my throat. "Not everyone has something like that in their lives. Something that gives them meaning and purpose and...joy."

She looks away again, back toward the flame that seems to capture so much of her attention. "Yeah, well, we all have to have something like that, right?"

"I wouldn't know. I drank my way through the first chunk of my life."

She frowns then, folding one of her legs until her foot is pressed to the inside of her thigh. "How'd you get through West Point without drinking?"

"Who says I did? Drank every night from plebe year on." It's an admission I've gotten more comfortable with. It's a choice I made. One I can't change now.

I can only move forward. Even if I still have no idea where I'm going, at least I'm not staying stuck in the past.

"Wow, and you never got caught? That's pretty impressive."

"My TAC caught me once. We'd just gotten out of the field at Buckner."

"And?"

"And he took my flask, took a long pull off it himself and told me if he caught me again, he was going to crush my nuts. So I made sure he never caught me again." I release a deep breath. "He never did. But the Highland Falls police were another matter."

She shifts then, folding her legs in front of her and turning to face me. "What made you stop drinking, if you've been drinking for all these years?"

She didn't ask what made me start. I suppose that's the harder question to answer. Then again, everything about being sober is harder.

I drag my hand through my hair again, then brace my elbow on my knee once more, looking at her. Trying to really see her, the woman across from me, rather than the fantasy I want her to be. "I woke up in an alley, leaning against a wall. I almost got arrested for arguing with some frat bro about Army football." Deep breath. "Shit. Talking about this fucking sucks." I grind the heels of my palms into both of my eyes.

I hear the rustle of her movement in the darkness. Then I feel her again, her shoulder pressed against mine, her knee resting alongside my thigh. She says nothing.

She doesn't have to.

Her body. Her warmth. Her simply being there.

It's more connection than I've had in my entire life.

And I suddenly have no idea how I have lived without it.

Nalini

IT'S a terrible thing to walk with someone through their life choices, especially the ones that have led them to me.

I can't say if I believe in some master plan. I'll never tell someone that things happen for a reason. I believe I am where I am supposed to be. It's my mantra. My purpose. My way of making sense of life. I don't know why, of all the buildings he could have ducked into to avoid the storm, he walked into mine. And I'm okay with that.

Because in this moment, sitting in the dark with only a flickering candle for light, a storm tearing at the walls over our heads, I know that I am here, now, because of him.

Because for some reason, our paths needed to cross. And somehow, I am exactly where I'm supposed to be.

It's what I've told myself since the fire consumed the vestiges of my confidence that I've spent the last three years of my life rebuilding.

It helps me make peace when the pain comes. And it always comes. Less these days than when I first started recovery, but it's a constant fear.

"So what did you do next?" I ask after a long silence.

"What do you mean?"

"You woke up in an alley. What came next?"

He glances over at me, his eyes a little darker than they were a few moments before. He swallows hard. His throat tenses and moves with the movement. "I went home. And spent a week in fucking hell trying to dry out."

I lift both eyebrows. "You didn't end up in the hospital? I had a good friend of mine go through the DTs. They're really awful."

"You have no idea. I thought I was going to die. Not figuratively, either."

"How long have you been sober?"

Another deep breath. "Two months." The words carry the weight of someone amazed he's saying them.

"Congratulations." It's funny that I can't come up with anything more profound than that simple word. It feels so inadequate.

"Yeah, well, habits are really hard to break."

"I have a mantra I use in class sometimes about habits."

He glances over at me, like the entire conversation is surprising to him. Like he's discovering something new with each breath. "I find myself deeply curious. I don't think I've ever heard a real mantra."

I smile because the part of me that wants a deeper connection to this man is wondering if he's just feigning curiosity to try and get closer to me. I don't get a sense of that, though. I find his interest genuine and I've seen enough fake interest from men who have fetishes about brown girls to have a pretty good idea what that looks like.

"It's from Gandhi. *'Keep your thoughts pure because your thoughts become your words. Keep your words pure because your words become your actions. Keep your actions pure because your actions become your habits. Keep your habits pure because your habits become your values. Keep your values pure because your values become your destiny.'*"

"That is really...profound," he says. I shift, brushing my knee against his thigh. The connection snaps between us, heat arcing across the narrow space. A brush of contact in the darkness. "And has it helped people?"

I lift one shoulder. "You'd have to ask people who use it. I find it has an effect on people who need to hear it. But that's the way with most mantras and yogic teachings."

He rests his elbow against one knee, cradling his head to watch me. "How on earth did you get through West Point with that attitude?"

I frown slightly. "What do you mean?"

"That's like nothing I've ever heard before in my life. I damn sure never heard anything like that when I was there. I just can't figure out how you developed a philosophy like that after being in the Army."

His question makes much more sense now. "Who says it had anything to do with being in the Army?"

"Touché." He touches his index finger to his brow bone.

"So has not drinking gotten any easier?" I need to shift the focus away from me. I'm curious about him—this man sitting with me in the dark as a storm races across the heavens overhead. This man who is serving as a shield I didn't know I needed, keeping fear of the storm and the dark and the fire at bay.

"Not really. Every day it's a battle to get out of bed and not grab a drink. I've thought about taking up heroin as a hobby to take my mind off the constant fucking craving."

"Heroin is a hell of a drug."

He glances over at me, one edge of his mouth curling slightly. "Was that a *Chappelle Show* reference?"

"Maybe. Depends on whether you approve or not."

He shifts, then angles his body toward mine. "Oh, I approve. I definitely approve. Especially of the subject change."

"Yeah, well, one can only handle so much personal pain and suffering before we shift back to more pleasant things."

"Like what?" His voice is low, his lips parted. There's something erotic about sitting in the dark next to a man who radiates both power and vulnerability.

"Like what's your favorite thing to do when you can't sleep?" His mouth is there, just there, a breath from mine.

"Read."

"Jesus take the wheel. You're a fucking unicorn."

His mouth twists sideways. "What do you mean?"

"You like filthy comedy. You read. If you tell me you like cunnilingus, we're getting married."

He chokes and breaks out into a full-bodied laugh. It looks like the laughter has caught him off guard, as though he's not used to the sensation.

"I'm not sure...what to say to that," he says after a moment. He leans his head back against the wall and closes his eyes. "There's really only one right answer, right?"

"Well, I'm sure there are a bunch of different ways you could answer that. But about half of them make this situation tremendously awkward."

He makes a noise deep in his chest. "We're already way past awkward, honey."

I rest my elbow on one knee, watching the flame in front of us, mirroring his position. Wishing we were in some other place and time and space. Letting his response hang between us. Letting it fill the silence and seeing where it takes us.

Silence can say so much more than words.

"So how did you get started doing yoga?" He hasn't moved from where his head is resting on the wall. His lips are parted, like he's trying hard to breathe deeply without me seeing.

"My paternal grandmother was a child of the sixties. She studied under B.K.S. Iyengar in India. My dad met my mom in college. She's a computer programmer. He's a psychologist. I grew up splitting time between the U.S. and summers in India." I pause, hesitating to admit how awful West Point was for me. "I didn't realize how homesick I would be at West Point. I started doing yoga again while I was there because it helped me feel connected with Hinduism, even a little bit. It grew for me from there. After I came home from

Syria and got out of the Army, I took some time and studied there myself. It was...it was time I needed."

He rolls his head on the wall and glances over at me. "I've heard of Castle Grayskull triggering some life-altering events in people but I've never heard of it being responsible for someone finding a new connection to their family."

"The Army changed a lot of things for me. Yoga was one of those things."

He's watching me. Slowly. Intently. It's so strange to see someone look so completely absorbed in what I'm saying. "What else changed?" A whispered question.

It's my turn to breathe in deeply, using the *ujjayi* breathing technique to calm the burst of nerves tangled in my chest. Restricting my breathing, I slow it down...deep and slow.

"I was working on a reconstruction project at an elementary school in Syria with the state department. I was attached to State as a military liaison. I was working on a counter intelligence operation under the guise of rebuilding the school..." My throat closes off, the memory of fear and anger and hatred burning through me like they did that day. It hasn't been nearly long enough ago for the heat and fear of that day to have faded. "Isis attacked the school. I got blown up in the process. When I got home, I needed some way to...heal. To unpack everything." This is all I can manage to push out past the blockage in my throat.

He's there then. Reaching for me. Pulling me close in a way that I haven't experienced in far, far too long.

And I let him, resting my head against his shoulder and sinking into the solid wall of strength and warmth that surrounds me. Some part of my brain recognizes that we've been in the basement long enough for his shirt to dry.

And still the storm is raging overhead.

Despite three years of work and of trying to accept what happened that day, there is still a part of me trapped in the past. Unable to let go of the certainty that I am somehow less than the woman I was before I went to war. That the scars burned into my body have seared a permanent place on my soul.

His palm is warm on my cheek, his whisper a caress across my skin. "I'm sorry. I didn't know. You don't have to say anything else."

This man is complicated. There is darkness in him. I know this. I can feel it in the shared memories each of us is terrified to reveal.

But that darkness is what draws me to him. What urges me to cross the space between us and press my lips to his. A gentle kiss. Meant to be more a balm than anything else.

It is anything but.

5

Caleb

I don't know how to kiss a woman.

At least, I don't know how to do it sober. I'm desperately afraid of screwing this up. Of pushing her away.

I only meant to offer comfort. The decision to pull her close was made out of pure instinct, something I wish someone had done for me all those years ago when I lost my mom. Maybe if someone in my life had taken the time to just hold the boy I'd been, I wouldn't have lost fifteen years of my life to destroying every good thing around me.

But the moment her lips touch mine something clicks into place inside me. Something intense and bright. Something that just *fits*. I open beneath her touch, flicking my tongue out to touch hers gently. Hesitant. Seeking connection.

Her tongue slides against mine —a tease, testing the space between us. It's as intense as it is needy and questioning. Her palms cup my face; her lips part against mine as she slips her tongue against mine. She's warm and slick and wet and utterly erotic as she touches a part of me that hasn't been touched in... I can't remember the last time I simply lost myself in the sensual pleasure of kissing a woman that wasn't twisted up with too much alcohol.

I don't think I ever have.

I stroke her tongue with mine, sucking gently on hers, drawing her closer, mimicking what I'd like to do to her body if she'd let me. Her crack about cunnilingus went straight to the juvenile delinquent part of my brain and I'm still wrapping my brain around the idea of her spread before me, her body laid out like a feast.

She makes a noise deep in her throat, something that sounds like the purr of a demanding kitten.

I ease back a little, nipping on her bottom lip, licking her gently to take the sting away from the bite. "That's...a good distraction technique you've got there," I whisper against her lips.

She smiles and it's warm and rich and melts me a little more. "I'm good at distractions."

"Yeah, you really are. I've —" I look away, realizing how fucked up it sounds to admit it—"I've never done this sober."

She narrows her eyes slightly, her lips curled faintly at the edges. "I feel like this is a really good opportunity to define our terms. Done what, exactly?"

"Kiss. Fuck. Be around a woman without being a total fucking asshole. How's that for starters?" The irritation snaps out of me before I can stop it. Before I can lash it back and keep it from crashing into the space between us and ruining the moment.

But she doesn't pull away. Doesn't even flinch at the venom in my voice or at the violence underlying it.

Her palm is cool where it lays against my cheek. Cool and soft, her fingers press against my skin. If I close my eyes, I can feel her heart beating through her fingertips. "You could have fooled me," she whispers.

"You're a very good liar."

She smiles against my mouth. "A cadet will not lie, steal, nor cheat."

"Yeah, well, you're not a cadet anymore."

"I still try to live up to that impossible ideal, even though I fail badly most of the time."

"Wow, talk about the biggest buzzkill in the entire world." I can't help myself from making the terrible joke.

She laughs. I'm starting to like the sound. It's something I'm completely unfamiliar with. Kind of like this ability to make someone smile.

I haven't done enough of that, either.

I'm usually on the other end of the spectrum when it comes to emotions. Usually, I'm doing or causing anger and frustration, coalescing somewhere near destruction.

Because I can't help the direction of my thoughts, because she is my confessor and my saving grace, I lower my head to hers. "Sorry," I whisper.

"For what?"

"Just...being entirely too awkward."

"Guys like you tend to have the opposite problem."

I stiffen. It's an automatic response, one I can't help. "What do you mean?"

She doesn't pull away. Her breath mingles with mine as she speaks. "You have all this hair and this scruff. Tattoos. All you need is a flannel shirt and some BCGs worn out of pure irony to be a hipster girl's wet dream."

"You find that nerdy hipster look attractive?" I might have to let the beard keep growing. And I bet I can find some damn glasses somewhere. Anything to keep the arousing feel of her fingers sliding along my jaw.

"I don't really have a type."

"Bullshit." A word without malice. "Everyone has a type. Or at least a type they think they have."

"And you're a master at this sort of thing because...?"

"I have spent the last fifteen years of my life in and around bars. I know the type of behavior that the female of the species exhibits."

"Correction. You know what the female of the species *who frequents bars* exhibits." She shifts away, resting against the wall so that her shoulder presses against mine once more. "You've got a selection bias in your sample, my friend."

"I don't even know what 'selection bias' is, but it sounds like something sexy when you say it." I lean back against the wall, too, pressing close to the warmth of her shoulder. "I'm dying to learn more."

The little flame has burned a crater in the middle of the candle's pale orange wax. I close my eyes for a moment, letting the sounds around us, and the conflicting sensations inside me, wash over me. Feel the cold of the stone behind me. The warmth of her shoulder against mine.

"Do *you* have a type?" she asks after a moment.

"I don't have a good way to answer that," I say softly. "Drunk me would pretty much go home with anyone who'd take me and *wow*, does that sound a lot more horrible when I say it out loud." I cover my mouth with my hand. Cold shame washes over me like the pin pricks of a thousand tattoo needles all at once. "I guess this is the part where I say I was always careful and have recently gotten all my shots?"

She makes a noise. "Good to know you're green on medical," she says. "I never in a million years would have thought that the Army's medical management system could ever be made to sound sexy." The ease in her voice is nice. Relaxing. I could listen to her reading a cereal box at this point and die happy.

"Clearly you didn't spend your deployment with the right people. We could make emergency nine-line MEDE-VACs sound sexy by the time we were done." I laugh, thinking of all the horrible pranks the guys used to play on each other.

"That's a power I could never have. The guys I deployed with were much more mature, at least in public." She smiles in the dark. "And yet somehow there was *Letters to Penthouse*-quality stuff written on the porta potty walls. Couldn't figure out how all the stuffed shirts at State could have such filthy minds."

"This is one of the strangest conversations I've ever had." I make a noise in the dark. "I'm enjoying it. Despite, you know, the threat of death from storm and all."

She smiles, resting her head against her knee, watching me warmly, the storm overhead forgotten, the storm between us simmering, just below a boil.

Nalini

It's easy to smile with him. "You can't explain why things like that are so funny to people who have never served."

He makes that noise again. That warm sound that comes from somewhere deep in his chest. "It's definitely something most folks don't understand."

He stills next to me but it's a comfortable stillness. I can't explain why I am so at ease with this man. I can't explain why the universe sent him into my studio at the earliest hours of the morning.

But I am grateful I am not alone. The dark, combined with the storm outside and the potential for fire... I'm not sure I'd walk away from all of this without a break in my view of reality if I were here by myself.

I'm long past questioning the way the universe works. And even though I haven't made my peace with what happened to me downrange, I'm working on it.

Working on finding meaning in hurt and the dark.

"After I got arrested, I thought for sure my military career was over. The Commandant looked at me and told me I wasn't West Point material. That I was a disgrace to the Long Gray Line," he says, not looking at me.

"Just for getting arrested?"

He lifts one eyebrow. "Um, you clearly went to a different institution than I did. Getting arrested was a cardinal sin to some of our peers. The minute I got in trouble, I was a pariah. Called a scumbag and told I didn't belong by my cadet chain of command."

"Yeah, some cadets aren't very forgiving when people make mistakes. But the best teacher is failure."

He makes a rough noise. "But the Supe...for some reason, the Supe gave me a second chance. I was a full year turn back."

"You had to do an extra year at Castle Grayskull? How did you survive?"

"I kept in touch with Eli. I tried to focus on not drinking as much so I wouldn't get caught. I didn't get sober but I kept it controlled and I managed to graduate." He releases a deep breath. "The Army really screwed up when they ran him out. He really is the best of us."

"Yeah, they really did," I say quietly.

He frowns and glances over at me. "You know Eli? I thought you said you'd never gone over to The Pint?"

"I haven't. Eli was a yearling in my company when I was a firstie."

Beside me, he's watching me intently in the faint candlelight. His eyes are piercing now, intense. Laser focused. "What's your last name?" His words are tighter than they were a moment ago.

"King."

"Holy. Shit." His eyes widen and he covers his mouth with his hand. "You were the regimental sergeant major my yearling year."

It's my turn to frown as I try to remember him. I chew on the inside of my bottom lip. "Does it make me a terrible person if I don't remember you?"

He curls one edge of his mouth. "Not really. I ran into people who remembered me but I have no idea who they were. There's only a handful of folks I kept in touch with. And by handful, I mean one in any meaningful way. Eli."

I tuck a strand of hair that's tickling my neck behind my ear. "I hope I wasn't too much of a jerk when you got in trouble."

He straightens one leg and bends the other. "You actually were the only person on the brigade staff to not be an asshole. Even if I did deserve it. I've had a pretty big fuck-you chip on my shoulder for a really long time."

I watch as he closes his eyes. "I was standing at parade rest outside the Commandant's office in my full dress uniform. You were arguing with another cadet—the regimental commander. I think his name was Peterson. He called me a piece of shit and you corrected him. You were so calm and poised. I remember thinking you were weak for defending me but a part of me was really grateful you stood up for me when no one else did."

Recognition dawns on me like the sun rising over the mountains, sliding into my consciousness. "Oh, wow, I remember that now. He was going off about how you were ruining his military grade for the semester and he should beat the shit out of you for being an arrogant little prick." I narrow my eyes at him. "That was you?"

He wears a sheepish expression and dear lord the man is sex on a stick. "Does 'I'm sorry for whatever I said' count this late after the event?"

I smile then, the kind of smile that says I'm not holding a grudge. Which is kind of amazing, to be honest. "You *were* kind of an asshole. You rolled your eyes when I came out to tell you to report to the Comm." I cup my cheek in one hand, studying him now, looking for the cadet he'd been.

"I was in charge of a ton of troublemakers my firstie year. You clearly didn't stick out that much." I've all but forgotten him in the intervening years. "Wow, small world. How did you end up in Durham?"

"I've been avoiding grad school for the last year and a half. My father pulled some strings to get me into the business school here, but I've been disappointing him regularly for the last decade or so. No reason to stop now." He releases a hard breath. "Though, if I'm going to get my shit together, I should probably go see Professor Blake sometime soon and do a metric shit-ton of groveling to see if she'll let me finish."

I shift then, crossing my legs in front of me and folding my hands in my lap. I move the candle a little farther away from us, needing the space from the open flame—a need I'm still pretending doesn't exist. "Wait. You just woke up after years of hard drinking and just...stopped?" That flies in the face of every bit of research I've done on trauma and addiction. "Most people don't just do that. They can't. Their habits are encoded too deeply into who they are."

"I won't say I just stopped. It's not like I just willed myself sober." He scoffs quietly. "It's been one hell of an identity crisis, if that's what you're getting at."

I glance down at the tattoos peeking out from the edge of his shirt-sleeve, finally daring to ask the question that I couldn't voice when I first noticed them. At the scrapes and bruises on his hands. At the two bandages encircling each wrist that I'm afraid to ask about. "Is that what these are?"

6

———

Caleb

The needle tears into my skin. A thousand times a minute, deliv-ering the pitch-black ink to a subdermal layer where it will stay. The second of two words is almost complete. The first still hurts like a son of a bitch.

～

I'm afraid to look over at Nalini. Afraid to see pity. Or judgment.

But I'm tired of being a coward. I lift my gaze to hers and find something...unexpected.

Compassion. Not pity. Not sorrow or judgment. Compassion.

"It's not what you think." My voice is thick. Rough. It's not, this time. And beneath the ink are the scars I'm trying to hide from the world.

I peel one bandage off, revealing the swollen red skin outlining stark Latin script.

Quo is on my left wrist. *Vadis* on my right.

She frowns. "What does it say?"

"It's Latin. *Quo Vadis*? It means 'where are you going' in Latin." I swallow. I didn't explain to Vega what the words meant when I asked him to ink them into my skin. But the dream that brought those words back to me was so real I'd woken up in tears after hearing my mom's voice again after so long.

And when I'd run after her, into the desert, I ran smack into Bruce.

I'd tried to forget it, throwing myself into work for the last twenty-four hours. But when I left Bruce's shop, I knew I couldn't go home.

"My mom used to ask me that when I was a little boy. There's an apocryphal story about St. Peter on his way to Rome before he's crucified. He becomes afraid and he turns to flee but Jesus meets him on the road and asks him 'Quo Vadis?' Where are you going? Peter finds the courage to return to Rome and well, we know how the rest of that story turned out."

She frowns. "No, actually, I don't. I know enough to know that's a Catholic legend but that's about it. St. Peter?"

"He was the first pope. Legend has it that he was crucified upside down by the Romans for preaching Christianity because he felt unworthy to die the same way as Jesus."

"You were raised Catholic?" There's a wariness in her voice.

"Carmella Acardo was my mother's name. That's about as Italian as it gets."

"Wait." She sits up. "Hold on. Then why were you surprised that I have so many aunts? Don't Catholics have big families?"

I look away. I didn't mean to bring up my family. "I have

a brother. We don't talk much. Haven't since my mom died. My dad shipped us off to military school about a year after she died. He couldn't handle the two of us on his own."

She's silent for a long moment. I can't tell her about Tony. I won't tell her what he did. What he allowed to happen.

The thing I tell myself I'm over.

West Point was tame compared to the *Lord of the Flies* bullshit that went on at that hell of a military high school.

Her palms are warm against my cheek as she slides them over my face. Smooth and softer than any other woman's hands. "I'm so sorry," she whispers. She's on her knees in front of me. The candlelight flickers in her deep brown eyes, flecks of dancing gold flame. "No one should ever be that alone. Not at twelve. Not ever."

I kiss her then because to do otherwise is to let the pain and darkness rise up and consume the rest of my soul. She's a light, liquid heat in my arms as I press my lips to hers with a need, a hunger. A simple touch won't do. I slide my hands over her ribs, tugging her toward me. She slips into my lap, her body pressed to mine in so many of the right places. Sensation sparks over my skin, little firecrackers of pleasure bursting against me.

Quo Vadis?

I don't have an answer to the question. Maybe I never did. Now, the words my mother used to call to me when I was younger are permanently etched into my skin where I can see them.

I offer up a silent prayer of thanks to the gods of yoga pants. The fabric is thin—so thin I can feel every crease of her flesh beneath my palms. There's an ache deep in my belly, a piercing need in my cock. An unfamiliar erotic arousal.

When you're sober, everything seems sharper and more focused. And in this moment, I feel every curve of her body. Every point of pressure where her heat presses against my erection. It's a fire that could consume me if I let it.

I want to let it. I want to lose myself in the sensation of her touch. The taste of her that has echoes of the scents from the studio upstairs. Sandalwood, maybe, and rose.

It sends me over the edge.

I'm not a religious man. At least, not overly so. But having Nalini in my lap, her body pressed to mine, her breath filling me, completes a piece of me that I've always known was missing but hadn't known how to find. Having her here is as close to a religious experience as I think I've ever known.

She pulls away slightly, nipping at the edge of my jaw until she gets to my earlobe. Her teeth scrape over the sensitive flesh and she traces the outline of my ear with the tip of her tongue. I shiver, closing my eyes and letting the sensation wash over me.

If I die in this moment, I will know true bliss, surrounded in sensation and pleasure and a feeling of being utterly *connected* to another person. I can feel her breathing as my palms press against her back, the rapid rise and fall of her breath as she presses her lips to first one eye, then the other, then to the center of my forehead before finding my mouth again.

"You are not alone," she whispers against my lips even as she slips her warm heat against my aching cock.

My eyes roll back into my head and I try not to embarrass myself by coming in my pants.

Her words slide up to the edge of the crevice inside of me. The gaping black abyss that was left behind when my life exploded in a firefight half a world away.

And they start to span the gap. Leaving me with a sensation of pleasure.

And a sense of *belonging* that I've been craving my entire life.

~

Nalini

I REST my forehead against his, absorbing the heat from his body, the energy.

The pain.

I can't say what made me crawl into his lap and press my body to his but there was something so lost in his words. His pain moved me, drew me closer. I needed to offer comfort the only way that felt genuine.

"No one knows what it feels like to lose someone that important to you, that young, unless they've gone through it. I can't tell you I know what you're feeling. I won't tell you I understand." My words are whispers against his lips. "But you are not alone."

His eyes are still closed. His breathing slow and steady.

It dawns on me that we are sitting in silence. That the storm overhead has moved away after hours of battering our world.

"I don't know what to say to that." His words are like something dragged over a grater; shredded emotion. After another moment he says, "I think the storm has passed."

It should hurt, his lack of response, but it doesn't because I can feel his fingers pressing into the small of my back. Deep pressure, telling me without words that he doesn't want to move.

I don't need the words. Words are empty without deeds.

His continued touch is enough.

"I think you're right." This was not a one-night stand but that's what it feels like now. Like we're severing a connection that had years to form instead of hours.

"I should go upstairs and check for damage." I don't want to move. I love the feel of his body against mine.

Sensation delayed, turned to torment.

He holds up his cell phone. "I can light the way."

I smile against his mouth. "That was pretty cheesy."

"I'm trying out different styles of sarcasm to see how they feel."

"Were you sarcastic when you were drinking?"

He closes his eyes, his fingers tensing against my back. "I was pretty much every dude bro stereotype you can think of."

"So...obnoxious and insecure?"

"Yeah. Among other things that I'd rather not process without heavy doses of alcohol." He brushes his lips against the pulse in my throat. I want to hold him there, to savor the sensation of his tongue on my skin. But I don't.

"I have to go."

"I know.

But neither of us moves for what feels like eternity.

I thread my fingers through his hair before sliding off his lap. My body cools instantly from the lack of his touch. His cell phone illuminates the area with harsh synthetic light as he blows out the candle. I mentally thank the squat fat candle for holding back the dark before this. It's a foolish thought but the softness of the candlelight made the moments between us more...real.

I lead the way upstairs to my studio. The power is back on upstairs but not down. "Must have snapped a breaker."

"Nalini..."

I glance over at him then follow his gaze. There's a tree where my car might have been if I'd parked it there today. Okay, maybe not an entire tree, but definitely a big piece of one. A massive oak branch taking up the entire space in front of my studio.

Part of it has crashed through the front window and taken down a good portion of the front wall and a chunk of the roof. Mala beads and singing bowls that I imported from India are scattered across the floor, mixed in with glass and debris. A part of my heart sinks down into my belly and I take a deep breath, trying not to cry. "Guess I'd better call the insurance company."

I feel him move before I hear him, his palm touching my back gently. "How can I help?"

His words, his touch is soothing despite the chaos at my center.

I take in the destruction. I'm mentally running through a checklist, praying that I made sure my insurance would cover acts of nature. "I can't...I need...I need some time to process everything." To call the insurance company, and then my studio members, to let them know everything is cancelled for today, at least. Probably for the rest of the week, or the month or...how long does it take to repair a building?

I drag my fingers through my hair, unable to process what I'm seeing. Unable to ask for help. Unable to think. To move.

To breathe.

His palm slips away from my back, and I feel an emptiness that I haven't felt since my mother told me she was disappointed in me for going to West Point.

I turn and look at him, surprised that he's leaving. "Where are you going?"

He pauses and looks back at me, a funny expression twisting his lips. He takes two steps toward me, pulls me close, threads his fingers into my hair. I expect the force of him against my mouth.

Instead, he rests his forehead against mine. Saying nothing. Saying everything without saying a word.

And then he's gone, disappearing through the branches of the downed tree and the debris.

Leaving me abandoned and alone.

7

Nalini

When a man walks into the destroyed remnants of a yoga studio with a chainsaw, most women do not think *oh, my hero*. No, most sane women would think *this is usually how horror movies start*.

But when that man is the man you just spent the last three hours with down in a dark basement, there are definitely dark and dirty thoughts happening.

"I'm not sure I've ever been so happy to see a chainsaw in my life."

He holds it up and offers a tired grin. "Give me some sugar."

I hold up one hand. "Okay wait, now you're doing *Evil Dead* lines?"

He shrugs. "I had a really boring tour in Iraq. Punctuated by a lot of *not boredom* but you...well, you get the idea."

He sets the chainsaw down and pulls a pair of work gloves out of his back pocket. "So where do we start?"

"Wait. Where did you get a chainsaw from?"

He tugs one glove on. "Bruce's shop is only a few blocks from here."

"And he has chainsaws in there?"

Caleb narrows his eyes at me as he pulls the other glove. "Do you know what a Maker Space is?"

"Not really."

"It's a fancy name for a crazy ass craft workshop. Power tools, 3D printers. Tech and electronics. Basically everything you could ever need for any type of project. Bruce has opened a couple of them. Home Depot has them. Encouraging people to get back into working with their hands. Craftsmanship. Tinkering. That sort of stuff."

I tip my chin, studying the man who looks so different from just a little while ago. "Who knew?"

He looks so rough and tired and yet he's still standing here, offering help that I didn't know how to ask for and have even less practice in accepting. I look at the wreckage of my shop. My studio. My entire life.

"Are you okay?"

I haven't felt this lost in so long. The feeling is still familiar, though. As though it never really went away after my deployment. "I don't know."

He takes a single step closer. I can feel the warmth from his body. Part of me wants to lean into him. To ask him to help me. To take this burden and carry it for me.

Because I am so tired all of a sudden.

"I don't know," I whisper again.

His hands are strong on my shoulders. I'm trying so hard not to fall apart right now. I have insurance. I can recover from this.

But right now, in this moment, I can find no sense of movement. No path through the debris.

No way out of the darkness.

I'm trapped. Just like I was back in Syria. Only there's no screaming. No crying.

Just emptiness. And sadness that echoes off the buildings like ambulance sirens.

I don't know how to ask for help. I don't know how to say the words. I want to. I know I need to. That I don't have to do this alone.

But the words are lodged in my throat.

His hands slip away when I don't move. I want to ask him to stay.

But I can't.

I close my eyes. Breathing.

Letting the cold, damp air from the hole in the glass flow into my lungs. *"Kali."*

"Who's Kali?"

I turn, having forgotten, however briefly, that I am not alone. "She is the destroyer. The protector. The giver of liberation."

"She sounds amazingly complicated." Caleb frowns, bending down to pick up a small white statue half-buried in the dirt from a plant that's having a really bad day. "Who is this?"

"Ganesh—he's the remover of obstacles." I take the statue from his hand, wiping the white elephant-headed figure clean and placing him on the counter. "The remover of obstacles." I smile then, the knot in my chest easing up as though I'm waking up from a deep sadness. "From death comes rebirth…"

My voice trails off as I survey the destruction. And I am suddenly seeing it not as destruction but as…freedom.

He lifts both eyebrows. "So the goddess of destruction is responsible for this? I thought you didn't believe in God."

I lift one shoulder. "I didn't say that. I said I struggle with it." I bite my lips, looking at the chaos around me. But I am no longer filled with loss and fear and sadness.

This path laid before me is daunting. Terrifying. And just because I'm starting to find meaning in this disaster doesn't mean...it doesn't mean the path will be easy.

"I guess...now is when I start salvaging what can be salvaged." I glance at the small white statue, who's fallen from the small shrine where I'd placed him the first day I opened my studio. "And see where the universe leads me."

"That's an awful lot of faith." He sounds skeptical. I don't really blame him.

"It's a coping mechanism," I say, more lightly than I feel. "It's that or I'm going to start drinking and I'm thinking that major construction projects don't go well with alcohol."

He glances down at the chainsaw at his feet. "That they don't."

~

Caleb

CHAINSAWS ARE THERAPEUTIC.

Honestly. It's just usually better to run them when you're not on an overtired high, when your wrists aren't throbbing from new tattoos.

But.

It's calming to cut through the tree branches. I watch Nalini drag them out of her shop even as I try to keep my hands from shaking from too little sleep and too much vibration.

The tree that's smashed through the roof and torn through half the building and its front window is a monster. Big enough to create a hell of a lot of damage and big enough that cutting it with a chainsaw is back-breakingly painful. Nalini's already filled two contractor bags with broken glass, cut-up tree limbs, and other debris.

But she looks as if she's taking everything in stride, to be honest. It's a little unnerving how calm she is now, after seeing her face when we emerged from the basement.

I don't know how she managed to switch gears so quickly. One minute, her breathing was fast and she looked like she was about to shatter like the glass in the center of her shop. The next...she was fine.

Okay, maybe not fine, but...a hell of a lot better than she had been.

I kill the chainsaw after the last chunk of the tree branch splits apart. She's made a neat stack of logs on the pavement outside.

She's not even sweating. What the shit is this? I'm ready to cry from my back hurting so bad from bending and sawing and she's just happily stacking wood.

"Maybe I need to get more into this yoga thing. You are peppy as hell for someone who's had their entire shop destroyed."

She drops another log onto the stack. "I love the smell of fresh cut wood."

I must be losing my mind. Or maybe I just need sleep. Probably both. "It sounds like there's a story there."

"I spent a summer in central Maine with one of my uncles. We had to split wood and toss it into the woodshed. It took a week, and I'd honestly forgotten about it until you started cutting."

I know she doesn't mean the words the way they come out but they slice at a memory, buried beneath tattoo ink. Resurrecting the time I cut at my own flesh and now sought to hide the evidence of that time beneath tattooed thorns and roses. At a time when I didn't know what to do with the pain eating away at my soul. A time before I found solace in a bottle and started killing myself slowly rather than attempting it all at once.

"Glad to bring about happy memories." I can feel my mood shifting and there isn't a damn thing I can do about it.

She shoots me a look but says nothing and I am a fucking asshole.

"Looks like you've got your hands full."

I look up at a voice attached to a big man with a big smile, stepping into the studio through the broken window.

Nalini smiles warmly. "I should have known you'd show up, Sam." She's not even done speaking when he grabs her and pulls her into a massive embrace.

She clearly knows him. I try not to feel jealous of the ease in how he moves, his confidence. He looks as if he's never met a challenge he didn't like. "Sam, this is Caleb. Sam and I were classmates. He's one of like six I actually still talk to."

I want to ask why she's so disconnected from other West Pointers but I don't. The time for intimate questions seems long past.

I suddenly miss the storm.

I reach out and take Sam's extended hand, determined to be civilized. "We've met."

She looks between us, waiting for one of us to clarify the situation, so I add, "Sam was the assistant operations officer in my battalion when I was a pain-in-the-ass lieutenant."

Sam grins and I'm mildly surprised he doesn't look like he remembers what a dick I was when we ran into each other at The Pint a few months back. "Still surfing unicorn porn?"

I was wrong. He does remember. And Jesus my face feels like it just turned fifty shades of red. "Yeah, about that..."

He shakes his head and slaps me on the shoulder. "I've heard you're working with Bruce now?"

I breathe out sharply. "Yeah. He took pity on me, and decided to put my rusty engineering skills to use."

Sam makes a noise. "That's good. Bruce...I've known Bruce a long time. I'm glad to see he's making use of your... unique talents."

I make a noise. "I guess I'll take that as a compliment."

"You should." His wide smile is a flash of white against his deep mahogany skin. His grin reminds me of the Rock's million-dollar smile and holy fuck I need to get some sleep. "So when were you going to call me?" he asks Nalini. "You know Sleet works at USAA, right?"

She sighs. It sounds familiar, like she's had this argument with him before. "I was working up to it."

I wonder what it feels like to have the kinds of friends you have patterns of conversations with, rather than stupid arguments about how much furniture you damaged during the previous drinking binge.

I pick up the chainsaw and step out of the studio. Nalini and Sam are discussing something about a warehouse and insurance claims, things I know somewhere between *jack* and *shit* about.

I'll take the chainsaw back to Bruce's shop. Tonight. This afternoon. Hell, whenever I wake up.

My apartment doesn't feel nearly as far away as it did in the middle of the downpour and holy hell I'm tired.

I slip out into the street, heading for home. It's better this way. That at least now, I can hold on to a memory of her without knowing that I've screwed everything up.

My tattoos are aching. My wrists feel wet and I really

hope it's sweat and not blood. I hope I haven't done any permanent damage.

I glance back at the light pouring out of the yoga studio onto the sidewalk beneath the dark gray sky.

And for once, I know where I am going.

Away.

Before I can do any real damage.

8
———

Nalini

The headquarters of Rossi Construction is in an old tobacco warehouse a few blocks away from the Durham Bulls stadium, halfway across the downtown area. I'm not entirely sure what I expect from this meeting but Sam and I go way back to West Point, and if anyone can help me figure out the design for the biggest gamble of my life, it's Sam.

The destruction from the storm six weeks ago has given me an opportunity. A chance to expand.

I've been needing to find a bigger space for about a year and a half.

And I've been stalling. Because...fear.

And now that choice has been made easier by...I don't know if it was pure chance or divine intervention but I'm taking the leap. And I am terrified.

That's where Sam comes in.

He is one of the few people I've kept in touch with from our class. He was an ace in our engineering classes back at

West Point. In the first few days after the storm, when I was surveying the wreckage of everything I'd built with my own two hands, Sam was a lifeline.

I'm deliberately trying not to think about Caleb. I'm grateful he helped with the chainsaw and the initial clean up. I'd wanted to offer to cook dinner or something as a thank you but when I turned around, he was gone.

No number. No good-bye. Just...gone.

I joked about Caleb being a single-serving friend but as it turns out, I guess that's exactly what he was. I'm not entirely sure how I feel about that, to be honest. But at least staying busy trying to get into the new building has kept me from dwelling on his complete disappearance.

I suppose it's for the better. I have far too much to do these days without worrying over someone I just met.

And now I'm sitting on an old building that I've just signed a mortgage to, as opposed to shelling out ten thousand dollars a month in rent.

I have absolutely no idea how I'm going to make this work and I've shut the studio down for a month. I've been doing classes out of an old conference room above the local bookstore but my clients are starting to grumble.

I have four weeks to get the warehouse ready for the first class, planned for the first night of Diwali.

A month to do a massive overhaul of a building that's most recently been home to a small but industrious and still illegal pot-growing operation. That venture came to an unfortunate end as a result of some overzealous cops.

Because why not, right? I inhale deeply, thinking of the destruction of my studio. It happened. It's time to use that destruction to create something new.

Besides, Sam will disown me if I chicken out. No matter

how much my anxiety about the finances is crushing my lungs, I will make this work.

I know I shouldn't be surprised when I walk into the Rossi building and am immediately encased in a sense of warmth. The floor is polished ebony concrete mixed with a silver and gold stain. Industrial lights illuminate the space. Black and white photos of old Durham during the Civil Rights marches decorate the brick walls.

The words Rossi Construction are burned into what looks like reclaimed barn wood.

The place radiates style and class.

In other words, classic Sam. Even his office space is clean and classy, sheltered behind a plate-glass window. He's arguing with someone on the phone. He grins when he sees me and holds up one finger. I'm happy to wait.

Once upon a time, I would have loved to have...ahem... gotten the finger from Sam. But that was before we both realized he and I would never be more than friends. He hangs up the phone and leaves the glass-enclosed office, his smile wide and welcoming against his dark skin.

"I still can't believe you never said yes when I asked you to yearling winter weekend," he says by way of greeting as he pulls me into a hug.

God, but it feels good to be held by one of my oldest friends. I forget, sometimes, just how important regenerating a real connection is.

"Yeah, well, why ruin a perfectly good friendship by screwing it up with dating?" I say, still smiling.

There's something warm and familiar about being around Sam. He was an ally at West Point when too few men were strong enough to stand up to the assholes who said women didn't belong. I was grateful to him then and I have more than a few reasons to be grateful to him now.

He leans back, his beautiful dark skin pierced by his brilliant smile. "I'm so glad you're finally doing this."

I suck in a deep inhale, holding it then pushing it out against the back of my throat in the *ujjayi* breath. "Let's not put too many expectations out into the universe. It sounds so much more intimidating when you say it out loud."

He ignores my anxiety. Not because he's insensitive but because he knows me well enough to know that I don't need any help in marinating in it.

"I've done some market research and looked at some of the leading names in yoga to get some ideas. I've come up with something that's a mix of Indian and contemporary American style." He motions for me to follow him through the wide open space, to a table constructed out of the same old barn wood as the Rossi Construction sign. A cream twelve-by-twelve folder on it stands out in stark contrast against the dark stained wood. "Before we start, can I get you some coffee? Tea?"

"Tea would be great, thanks." My eyes are drawn to the folder and he grins.

"Go ahead and flip through it. I'll be right back."

I sink into a rich leather couch. My palms are slick as I reach for the folder. Everything about this is terrifying. Expanding into my own space is everything I've ever wanted but it's such a huge risk. Most yoga studios don't survive six months and if they do, they barely scrape by.

I've been going strong since I started two years ago and I'm running out of room because my classes keep filling up. These are good problems to have but I've been resisting the move. The storm merely forced me into a decision point that I'd been avoiding.

If I want to continue to serve as an entryway for people to learn about the Dharmic way of life associated with yoga,

I need to change. To reach back to the country where I spent so many summers and bring something authentic to American yoga, like Swami Vivekananda did a hundred years ago. Guru Iyengar's teachings are helping me stay grounded in authentic traditions. But to survive in this marketplace, I have to adapt. To create a fusion between East and West that somehow stays true to both.

It's a massive, massive risk. People in America tend to think of yoga as a fitness program, and for some people that's fine. But commercialism has clouded the meaning and the spirituality behind it.

Unfortunately, I'm part of the commercialism, despite wishing it were otherwise. I tell myself that at least I'm trying to make it something deeper, even if people do still have to pay for my classes.

I've been heading back to my roots for a long time. This is just another step along the way, one the universe apparently decided it was time for me to take.

Sam settles onto the couch next to me, handing me a mug that looks handmade. The tea smells rich and earthy and faintly of cinnamon.

I flip open the folder and I'm hit with a sense of…rightness.

"We're going to stain the concrete to warm the space up. We've got a couple of designs you can do in the floor but I think large colorful mandala designs would strike the right tone. Painting the walls will brighten it. We don't have to replace most of the windows, which will save you a ton of money, but we should paint the trim and redo the ledges. I emailed your Uncle Prakash in Mumbai and he's already lined up shipping for the fabrics for the window hangings as soon as you make a choice. That will save you painting time."

The design is incredible. He's somehow managed to overlay a multicolored mandala in the middle of a stained concrete floor at the entrance. The walls are a pale powder blue, a color that strikes me as the color of Shiva. A tapestry of the elephant god Ganesh hangs on one wall. Between two windows in the main studio hangs a spoked wooden wheel —a symbol of the Buddha.

The details he's found. I'm speechless, staring at his design as though my space isn't currently a rundown warehouse filled with cobwebs and boxes of discarded dreams from the previous owner.

"Sam...this is amazing."

He presses on, as if I'm not sitting there on the verge of happy tears. "The good news is that you can do a ton of this work yourself, like you wanted." He flips the page. "This is the part where you'll need some help."

He lays out the designs behind constructing dividing walls, a task which is both necessary and intimidating. "You've got two options if you want to create a heated space. You can build it into the space, and that means building walls and a ceiling and running ducts for the heat. Or you can make the heated studio in the basement. You know which one I recommend, right?"

"Yeah, the idea of building walls by myself doesn't sound too appealing." Then again, neither does building the heated studio in the basement. "Is there any other way?"

"There's the possibility of simply dividing the space in two but you'll have to have an electrician put the air on two separate circuits. You don't have to decide immediately but it's a big decision you have to make relatively early on." He flips the page. "The flooring inside the studios is bamboo. Sustainable and incredibly durable, and this way your members aren't doing yoga on concrete or nasty mats that absorb bacteria." He glances over at me. "You're good with installing flooring?"

"Yeah. I put together my first studio. I can handle flooring, painting, and installing shelving. Walls, though…"

"If you take my advice and make the basement into two separate spaces, it'll make the upstairs a lot cleaner and easier. I've got a team that can help with the framing of the necessary dividing walls in the basement. And we've got to clear the building of lead paint. I've got the permits and hired a team. They're ready to get started once you get everything cleared out."

I breathe out again. "I'm…this is real. This is really happening."

He grins over at me. "You deserve it. You know that, right?" He's said that to me before. Many, many times.

It's hard to hear but I learned a long time ago not to ignore Sam Rossi when he tells you something. His faith in the people around him is…astonishing.

I look down at the designs. "There's so much that could go wrong."

"Everything already did, with the storm. This is cake for someone with your stubbornness issues." He smiles wickedly, lifting his coffee to his lips. "Consider me your fairy construction godbrother." He slides an invoice toward me. "Wholesale discount on the flooring ready for once we've cleared the building for reconstruction. You'll have one large area that remains stained concrete and the smaller studios will be wood. The heated studio is going to take a little longer but you should be able to get this done in two weeks, no problem at all, leaving two weeks for cleanup and any errors. I'm assigning Bruce Forsythe to work with you on this. He's doing it pro bono because we're all about supporting a fellow veteran-owned business."

"Yeah? That's really awesome." For a fleeting instant I think the name Bruce should mean something to me but exactly what slips out of my grasp. I am not going to say no to help. It's my biggest weakness and I remind myself to say yes. "My entire staff is working on this. I shut the studio down so we can focus. Thanks be to Mother Nature and all that."

I study the floor plan. There's a small area set off for the entrance and a desk edged with stone detailing. "People will have to walk through the retail area to get back to the studios," I murmur.

"That's smart business. Helps with impulse purchases. And here you'll have a small café. Uncle Ganesh has come through again with tea being shipped from the Mumbai Tea Company. You'll have a studio that no one in the area can match for uniqueness and authenticity, and that's something that people are willing to pay for. Cinnamon Chai's manager is interested in renting space from you if you decide you want to farm the café out rather than run it yourself. Seeing how you'll own the whole building and all that, bringing on renters would be a smart financial move."

I sip the tea, the warm cinnamon warming the back of my throat. "I'll think about it. I'm honestly not sure I'm ready to turn this into an entirely commercial space. I'm on the fence about so many things. I haven't even started thinking about expanding the retail section. I wish I could run this place without it but, yay capitalism and all that, right?"

"You can support fair trade products from Mumbai and support local vendors here. You can do this in keeping with your philosophy." God, but he says that with so much confidence and calm. Like the world is just going to make this dream a reality.

I glance over at him. "Sam, thank you so much for this. I can't even tell you how amazing this is. I don't know how you did it but this is exactly what I wanted."

"To new spaces and old friends." He clinks his mug against mine then pins me with a look. A look that says he's about to ask a question I don't want to answer. "Speaking of friends...What was going on with Caleb and the chainsaw?"

I smile. Only Sam could make such a personal question so not threatening. "He was caught in the storm and we ended up taking shelter before the worst of it blew through. He...stayed the entire time then showed up with this miracle chainsaw. Then he...vanished. I wanted to write him a thank you note for his work with the chainsaw but he was just...gone."

"So you spent a couple of hours trapped in a basement with a complete stranger who then shows up with a chainsaw, helps you remove a shit-ton of big ass tree and then vanishes like a chainsaw-wielding fairy godfather?"

"Well, it does sound a little crazy when you put it that way." I sip my tea. "Caleb was...interesting. And fascinating. Did you know he's an Old Grad? He was one of my problem cadets, apparently, our firstie year."

"I didn't know you knew him." That seems to have caught his attention. "We were in the same battalion. He was a serious fuck-up as a lieutenant."

"I think this is the first time I've ever heard you say anything...harsh about anyone."

Sam narrows his eyes at me. "He... Let's put it this way. He didn't have his shit together." There are so many different ways I could interpret that statement. "But..."

"You don't need to finish that thought. This is going exactly nowhere. I don't know where he lives. I don't have his number. He was helpful and, well, I don't need any distractions from work. Not this month, anyway."

He shakes his head. "No one dies thinking 'wow, I really wished I'd worked harder'. You need to take some space and time for you, Lini."

I shake my head. "What makes you think he's part of that space and time?"

He shrugs and damn it, I wish he wasn't so damn nice all of the time. "I can hope that maybe someone will come along and help you...feel like you again. I know how important your studio is and I know you can get there without needing to depend on anyone." He grips my shoulder. "But this life is too short to go through it alone. And if I had to bet on one thing, it would be that the universe didn't put him in your basement for him to disappear on you without a reason."

I roll my eyes and bump my shoulder into his. God, but I love this man. Why couldn't my own family be as supportive of me and my life as this man I love like a brother? "You should write novels, Sam, because that is the sweetest thing anyone has ever said to me."

"Look. Just...never mind. Let's talk lighting."

I'm not sure why he changes the subject but I'm grateful. I can handle the teasing. I can handle the urging me not to work so hard.

I can't handle the worry I see in his eyes when he looks at me.

Because it makes me feel incomplete. Like my healing from the attack in Syria isn't over.

I want it to be. I want to be me again. Whole. And I want to get that way on my own terms. I don't want to be fatalistic and depend on the universe. I don't want to challenge the universe to destroy something in my life.

I just want...to be myself again.

~

Caleb

BRUCE DOESN'T DO COUNSELING. Which is definitely not what I expected when he dragged my ass out of that alley a few months ago. I fully expected some hippie group therapy meetings about finding a higher power and admitting you have a problem.

Granted, he did sort of get me to confront that I had a massive fucking problem when I was in the throes of the DTs.

Kind of hard to go *yep, everything is fine* when you can't stand up without heaving your guts up and are pretty sure there's one of those little alien things running up and down your spine.

I deeply regretted any life choices that involved binge-watching the *Aliens* movies before I dried out.

I do not recommend that. At all.

But I survived and now I work in one of those Maker Spaces where people come to use the 3D printer or the tools. My job is weird. He doesn't ask me about staying sober. Doesn't ask me about how late I stay at the shop to avoid not sleeping. He can see when I close the shop up at night and set the alarm. He trusts me to shut it down at midnight per his instructions.

No, we work on furniture, we talk about life, the universe and everything in between. But in the spaces between actual meetings, I'm on my own, working on whatever furniture project needs to be done and trying to find the pieces of me that are either still missing or still being reconstructed.

It's the strangest therapy I've ever even conceived of. And oddly enough, I'm doing okay. I've managed to stay sober. Almost four months. Every day, it's a struggle. Some days are harder than others.

But working with my hands is good. I like it a hell of a lot more than sitting in classes at business school, where my mind wanders and questions the futility of it all.

Building takes a concentration. A flow.

It turns out, I like working with my hands. I guess I forgot that after my mom died.

I walk into Bruce's office bright and early. Funny thing about not sleeping: you're always the first one at work. His office looks like a construction foreman's office—a rickety metal desk covered with scattered paperwork and folders and a thousand misplaced sticky notes. A coffee maker, with a pot that hasn't seen the inside of a scrub pad in this decade at best, leaves the room filled with the smell of slightly burnt coffee. The floor, though—the floor is what busts me up every time I walk into his office.

It creaks. The kind of old wood creaking that is guaranteed to announce the killer is approaching during a horror movie. I guess this is what it feels like to walk into a waking dream where you're not entirely sure you're going to hit a fantasy or a nightmare.

Maybe they're one and the same.

Today, though, something stops me at the door. Maybe I'm overtired. Maybe I'm just cranky, but standing in the doorway to Bruce's shop, I'm hit with a sense of familiarity that physically hurts. I can practically hear the gentle tinkling of the wind chimes in the corner of the shop. The smell of fresh sawdust is clean and crisp and damp. I am suddenly ten years old, standing in the doorway of my grandfather's woodshed where he used to spend hours a day building things and drinking away memories of Vietnam.

It was a memory I'd long forgotten until just now. One I'd apparently buried after I lost my mom and the life we had.

Bruce strolls out, his pepper-gray hair covered by a red bandana that's striking against the sun-damaged tan of the skin on the top of his head. "Was starting to wonder if you were going to show up."

"Isn't there a standing threat to hunt me down and kill me if I don't?" He reminds me of my old first sergeant. Don't get it twisted—he will show up at my apartment. He's done it.

So I try to make sure I show up every day.

"Yeah, well, glad you took me seriously." He's gruffer than usual today.

It's easy to fall into the bullshitting that soldiers are famous for and that I find I miss something terrible. There's something comforting about talking shit to the men to your left and right when you're sitting in the woods in the cold and the dark.

"What are you working on today?"

"We've got a new job. Come on; I'll show you real quick before we have to be where we're going."

I have no idea how this is supposed to work. I have no idea how I got here except that Bruce sat me down and told me that being a drunk fucking sucked and ordered me to come to his woodworking shop. Said I looked like I needed something to do with my hands.

At the time they'd been shaking because I'd needed a drink, so I guess he wasn't too far off.

We walk past two-inch thick, long wooden planks spread out on a workbench. They're at least eight feet long.

They're dingy gray and look like they've been out in the woods for far too long.

"This is going to be a table?" I'm skeptical, to say the least.

He runs a gloved hand over the edge. "Funny thing about wood. You can beat it up. You can burn it. You can warp it. But if you apply enough pressure and heat, you can remold it. Shape it into something beautiful."

He sounds like a lover caressing his partner's skin.

"So how does this work?"

"Well, first we're going to scrape off the old. Rough sandpaper to take off the outer layer that's protected the inner layers."

This is quite possibly the strangest therapy I could have imagined. But whatever. He's not wrong. I need something to do with my hands.

"But this piece is warped. It doesn't even sit flat on the table."

He grunts and points to a furnace-looking thing. "That's what the kiln is for. We apply heat and pressure, and it'll be flat as the day it was planed."

Okay, then.

I follow him out to his truck and get in, glad I actually was able to eat breakfast before I came to the shop today. Food is still challenging sometimes. For several seconds neither of us speak as he drives.

"So did you get into woodworking first and the saving of souls came second, or was it the other way around?" I ask as he pulls to a stop in front of a flashing railroad crossing sign. I find myself suddenly needing to know why he found me and kicked my ass into sobriety. Funny how I never questioned it before now.

He shoots me a quick look. I can't decide if it's *fuck you, smart ass* or something else.

I shrug and watch a passing train. "Just curious," I mumble. I can't figure out what his problem is today.

Bruce drums his fingers on the steering wheel. "I was one of the thousands who were told 'thank you for serving' after Desert Storm and then given my marching orders when the Army decided to downsize. I tried a couple of corporate jobs but they just didn't work. Got myself divorced because I was drinking too much and pretending I was still a stupid enlisted guy. My uncle scooped me up—kind of like I scooped you up—and taught me how to keep my hands busy. So I think the woodworking came first. And I don't know a damn thing about saving souls."

"So you just woke up one day and decided that scooping up random drunks and putting them to work with things that can dismember them was a good idea?"

"Well, this ain't the Army anymore, so I can do my own risk assessment. And if I really thought you were going to show up drunk, you'd be drying out somewhere else first."

I shake my head and say nothing, the unexpected jab at my struggle with sobriety slicing at me. I like Bruce. I can't say why because he's somewhat cranky and likes to drop surprises in people's laps without warning. But today, he's off. Grumpier than normal.

"So, how goes the not-drinking thing?"

Ah, another question I don't really know how to answer. "Good. Except for the not-sleeping part."

He makes a noise. "I think I've got a solution for that."

I glance over at him and say nothing. I don't know where we're going.

But I think I'm okay with that.

9

Nalini

The old Calhoun warehouse is prime real estate. It's nestled between the already gentrified area around the Durham Bulls stadium and the old tobacco district that's still being restored one building at a time, and somehow I snagged a bargain that should have been illegal. Well, given that the previous owners were using it to grow pot...it pretty much was illegal.

I'm not complaining, even if I do think they need to legalize weed, especially for medicinal uses. Who knows; maybe if I can make a go of things with the yoga center and they legalize marijuana, I can expand into medicinal herbs.

I grin. I've clearly spent far too much time in a college town. Though, to be honest, I've never really had a problem with other people smoking weed. I'm pretty sure my paternal grandmother was smoking all the time when she was studying yoga. Not that that was sanctioned by Guru Iyengar.

Looking at the job in front of me, though, I might need to start. Standing inside the entrance at the top of a flight of red brick stairs, I survey the sheer magnitude of work ahead of me. My chest tightens.

Everything has to go. There are places where the floor is caved in, revealing a dark chasm some people might know as the basement, but I'm thinking *aka* the stuff of nightmares. A good chunk of floor will need to be reframed and replaced, but if Sam's idea works, that hole in the floor near the stairs is going to be opened up to the two basement studios.

It's daunting, to say the least.

There are rows of tables and hanging lights. The cops already took all the weed – at least I hope they did. I really don't feel like dealing with disposing of any remains. The only thing I was definitely able to confirm about the building was that it had been used strictly for pot, not by meth dealers cooking their product. If there had been meth in here, I might just as well burn the place to the ground. The chemicals left over from that process are a whole new level of toxic.

The same cannot be said for the product of the recently convicted weed growers, aka the former tenants, however. That's the biggest reason I was able to get the property so cheap—the bank wanted to recoup their investment and anyone occupying the space and paying for it is better than anyone who is not. I have no idea why the former owners were growing weed in the middle of downtown Durham, nor do I want to know how or why they ended up getting busted.

However, that means I'm now the proud owner of weed-growing equipment that the police didn't confiscate for some reason.

Maybe I should hold on to it for when they finally legalize marijuana. The thought makes me snort and the sound echoes in the wide open space. This is North Carolina. They'll vote for a Democrat before they legalize pot. At least the people outside of the Triangle would. Those in the Triangle—the area anchored by North Carolina State, the University at Chapel Hill, and Duke—with Raleigh and Durham in there, too—well, they've definitely got some pro-weed tendencies.

Sunlight spreads across the dusty floor, filtering in through massive windows colored with dust and age. The effect is somewhat haunting.

I glance over at the caved-in hole in the floor. It's not that far from the stairs and the light filters down into it then disappears like it's some kind of black hole sucking up everything. "This is how horror movies start," I mumble. Maybe Sam is right and I should hire someone to do this for me. I'm not a big fan of cellars and the one below me seems like the perfect place for some high-powered psychopath to have buried some bodies.

And wow, are those some comforting thoughts. It's really the mark of complete insanity how I'm standing here freaking myself out.

What I need to do is get some damn work gloves and get started.

But that's the problem with massive projects: they're overwhelming.

My phone vibrates in the back pocket of the beat-up jeans I wear for work when I'm not in yoga pants. I frown looking at the screen, then answer on speaker phone. I hate holding phones up to my ear. "I wasn't expecting to hear from you so soon."

Stephanie White and I will never be friends. At least not

any time soon. She's the executive director of the Wellness Center on campus and she and I used to be very close. I trusted her and she connected me with more than one young student who was struggling with a variety of issues. She linked me up with Kelsey Ryder, who has been a regular at my studio since she arrived on campus.

But Stephanie and I have recently parted ways over her contracting with a company for the new yoga studio at the Wellness Center that I vehemently disagree with and...yeah, unfortunately, I'm taking it personally.

It's not easy for me to ignore when someone advocates for a yoga program that denies everything that makes yoga what it is, and instead turns the practice into a bastardized fitness program for rich women in hundred-dollar yoga pants. It's not like I was going to start holding Hindu ceremonies there. Though I would have, had they asked me to.

I take a deep breath. I can do that in my own space. The door closing on campus means the one here, in this warehouse, has opened. I can do this.

"I wasn't expecting to reach out, if we're being honest." Her voice is polished and smooth in a way that mine will never be. She reminds me so much of a younger Princess Leia before she was General Organa. Poised. And she's always three steps ahead of everyone around her. "But I'd like your assistance on something."

I bite back a smart-ass comment. I don't believe in Hell but I briefly wonder if they're holding the Ice Capades there.

Then I decide the universe doesn't need me burning any more bridges. I don't have nearly enough to spare. "I'm listening."

She makes a quiet noise, barely audible. "Despite our differences about the Wellness Center, I would like to invite you to a panel on multiculturalism in a secular age, on campus next week. The Wellness Center has been dealing with a lot of...friction on campus from the Indian student body —"

"Wait, hold on a sec." And there goes my self-control. I suck in a deep breath and hold it before I speak in a deliberate, epically false calm. Lying is sometimes a life skill. "You shot down my proposal for an Iyengar center on campus—which has a sizeable Indian student body, remember—to replace it with some bastardized commercial practice that is so patently ripping off Indian culture and is widely known in India for problematic proselytizing that targets the vulnerable, and you want me to come participate in a panel? To what? Help soothe things over for the mess you and the Board of Directors made?" There I go, breathing deliberately again. But I don't yell. I don't even raise my voice. No matter how badly I *really* want to. Releasing the fury gripping my lungs would be *so* cathartic.

"There's no way I can convince you that decision was out of my hands, is there? The studio we ended up contracting with is connected to a powerful alumni family. This is way bigger than you and me, Nalini."

I smile coldly, despite knowing she won't be able to see it. "It's not that it went to someone else. It's that it went to this particular company. I warned you and the board that this company has a problematic history in India, but you didn't want to hear it. And now you want me to be the token brown woman to help you out of the completely foreseeable backlash that I warned you about."

"I understand you're angry and you have a right to be."

Honest to god, I almost snap at the patronizing tone in her voice. It's a miracle my head hasn't exploded.

"Look, there are some very important people who are highly upset about the Wellness Center and we'd really like your help to start a conversation. To get people to listen to both sides of the issue."

I'm clinging to self-control by a thread. A frayed one. "Look, Stephanie, I appreciate you reaching out but there isn't really a conversation here. The program you all contracted with has been practicing cultural erasure in India for over a decade. The Indian student affairs board is aware of this and, well, if the board wanted to fix this, they'd find someone else—hell, *anyone* else—to provide the yoga services."

"There are legal reasons why we can't do that. No one foresaw the students being as angry as they are." Stephanie sounds exhausted and once upon a time, I would have felt sympathy for her. But I'm tired of doing the work of cleaning up people's messes when I warned them this would happen.

"Um, I did. And I submitted—in writing—why this particular yoga company was a terrible idea," I say. "Just because the board assumed that I was being—I believe their words were 'reactive' and 'hypersensitive'—because I was 'too close to the issues', doesn't make it my responsibility to help now."

I'm calmer now. Hahaha, no I'm not.

She pauses, the silence dragging on for so long I glance at the phone to make sure she hasn't hung up on me. "Nalini, for what it's worth, I tried to get them to consider your perspective."

Her words are a slap, a vicious reminder that I am and always will be an outsider at this elite school, just like I was back at West Point. "I know you believe that but I saw your email minimizing my argument."

"I'm hoping someday you'll understand the compromises you have to make when you're steering an organizational ship."

I press my lips together. "And I hope I never get the opportunity if that means I have to betray people who trusted me."

"I'm sorry you feel that way."

"Me, too." I end the call before I say something I'll regret. I shouldn't be so hostile about the takeover at the Wellness Center with a variant of yoga that is pure bullshit. It's definitely not very yogic of me.

But since the destruction of my studio in the storm, everything has been off-center for me. I'm unmoored, unbalanced. Adrift even as I try to steer my life back on course by focusing on what I'm trying to build here.

And the call with Stephanie, asking me to do work that I've already done when they didn't listen to me the first damn time—

I'm shaking with anger at being reminded of the crushing defeat at the campus advisory meeting a few weeks ago.

It wasn't even defeat, actually; it was a dismissal. It was being told I was being oversensitive because someone did something I disagreed with. Like someone using your culture to destroy your culture is something to just be calm about. I kick at an empty bucket, only to realize as my toe collides with the unmovable object that it's filled with concrete or something damn close.

My profanity-laced verbal explosion echoes through the dust-filled space.

"Well, that's one way to start the day."

I scream again for good measure and try not to jump out of my goddamned skin.

Because my single-serving friend has just scared the shit out of me.

~

Caleb

I REALLY HAD no idea what her greeting would be, but a full-blown scream wasn't really the reaction I was going for.

She's been a constant presence in my mind since the storm. In my apartment as night slithered across the floor, I'd think of her: sitting with her during the storm, riding it out. Feeling her lips brush against mine.

Thinking about her whispering *you're not alone* as I sat in my empty, silent apartment.

God, but it's good to see her. In full daylight, even in a full-on bout of anger, she's stunning. Vibrant. The bright pink T-shirt she's wearing makes her dusky copper skin glow. Her cheeks are flushed and hot damn is she sexy as hell when she's pissed.

"Do you always sneak up on people?"

Maybe that glow isn't about vibrancy, I suddenly think; *it could be about anger*. It wouldn't be the first time I've made that mistake.

I'm torn between trying not to laugh at the obvious wounding of her pride and actual concern that she may have broken her toe. "Do you always rage-kick buckets when you get off of particularly passive-aggressive phone calls?"

She pauses and I can practically see her debating whether she should be pissed at that response, or something else. She releases a heavy sigh and a tiny smile creases the edge of her lips. "You heard that, huh?"

"Anyone could have caught that. Your voice was dripping with it." I glance down at her toe, that she's still favoring. Standing inside the doorway of the warehouse, all I can think about is how great it is to see her again.

It takes a minute to remember my manners—that I am not a mouth-breathing drunk who is going to spend the night staring at her tits while I pretend to be interested in what she has to say.

I go for something basic. Simple. "Are you okay?"

She's grinding her teeth as she sets her foot down. "Yeah. Mostly pride at this point."

"Yeah, well, pride might need to get its happy ass to the emergency room unless those boots are steel-toed."

She tips her head, shifting her weight to the damaged foot. "What do you know about steel-toed boots?"

"I know enough to know that if you're wearing them, you might not have broken your foot. Then again, maybe if you were wearing them you wouldn't have been tempted to kick the bucket. Literally, not symbolically."

She takes a few steps and while she's pretty steady, she's still favoring her foot a little bit. Watching her, I don't think it's broken but it could be. Broken bones don't always show up immediately. Weird things I learned at combat lifesaver training back in the Army.

"I'm working on my temper," she says dryly.

I press my mouth into a flat line and barely avoid scoffing. "Looks like it. I thought you were supposed to be some yogic master with inner peace or some shit."

She braces her hip against a dusty windowsill and folds her arms over her chest. She's still breathing hard. My attempt to distract her from the phone call doesn't appear to be working. "Nothing about being a yogi says 'perfect'."

"That doesn't actually surprise me." I lift one eyebrow

and try to play it cool because this is the longest interaction with a female that I've had sober since...well, since our last interaction. "I was scolded at Whole Foods last week by a woman who claimed I interrupted her *chi* when I reached around her meditative pose in front of the Brussels sprouts."

"That did not happen." Finally, she cracks a grin. "Wait, you eat Brussels sprouts?"

"Oh, yes it did and yes I do. She was waiting for the universe to help her pick the right sprouts for her tofu."

She is the only person I can remember in recent time who has laughed at my terrible attempt at humor. I'm finding my footing. Slowly. One day at a time and all that.

I'm not entirely sure how I feel right now. There's something warm in the vicinity of my heart watching her visibly regain control of her emotions.

"That is the most hipster thing I've ever heard." She's still smiling. And dear lord, she's stunning. Standing in the early morning daylight, dust floats around her head like a sparkling halo.

It's not healthy, standing here and letting myself feel these things. I close my eyes and wait for the inevitable guilt to wrap around my chest and squeeze the air from my lungs.

But after a moment, I realize she's still talking. And I'm still breathing.

I guess it's a day for miracles, after all.

She takes a step toward me. My breath catches in my throat. I am frozen, anchored in place as she steps closer, close enough that I can see the dusky rose flush to her skin.

Her palm is warm on my chest. "How have you been? With everything?"

It is the kindest question she could have asked. "Still sober, if that counts."

She smiles warmly, the heat from her fingers slipping beneath my skin to warm my soul. "That's a pretty big deal."

"Yeah, well. Let's not jinx it."

Her fingers flex against my chest. "It's good to see you." Her voice is liquid honey, smooth and rich and deep. "I wanted to thank you. For your help with the storm, but you disappeared."

"I figured you were busy after the storm. I didn't want to get in the way or anything." I look around at the warehouse, needing to distract myself from the urge to return her touch. "So you giving up on yoga and taking up growing weed?"

She breathes out in that way that she does that I've been unable to get out of my mind since the storm. "Not exactly." She turns away, looking at the boxes and dust and overall disorder. "CliffsNotes version: previous owners were growers. Got seized by the cops. Since the studio was almost a total loss from the storm, I basically used the insurance money and a little bit of my savings to get into this place with a manageable mortgage. And so I have a month and a very strict budget to get this place converted into a functioning yoga studio."

I drag my hand through my hair and dare to take a single step closer. "I guess that's why I'm here then."

"Oh... You work with Bruce and Sam hired Bruce to work on this." She glances over at me. Her gaze is warm now, not filled with anger from the phone call, as realization dawns. "I've never met any of Sam's people."

"Bruce isn't one of Sam's people but apparently he works a lot of subcontracted jobs for him." I point over my shoulder. "Makes my engineering degree from West Point useful, I guess."

I avoid looking at her, trying to ignore the hole in the

floor off to the left of us. Instead of a normal staircase leading into the basement, the wood planks have been ripped away, leaving a ragged chasm that looks like a stairway to Hell.

I'm waiting for a killer clown to crawl out of that son of a bitch and wishing I had something a hell of a lot sharper than a Leatherman on me.

In which case, I'd be going to jail for arson because *fuck that shit*.

"That sounds horrifying," she says quietly.

"What, dead clowns?"

The moment I speak, I realize that I've drifted off and answered her comment with a complete non sequitur.

"Not sure how we got from engineering to clowns, but okay." She lifts both eyebrows, her lips parted with a slight crease at the edge.

"Do you have something against clowns?"

A little line furrows between her brows. "I thought we were talking about construction?"

"Oh. Yeah. Sorry. I wandered off. Mentally." *It happens*, I want to tell her.

But I don't. Because I can barely get myself out of bed every morning and I'm confident she can look at me and see every single way I'm beyond saving.

Instead, she smiles and looks over at the hole in the floor, folding her arms over her chest. "I don't know about you, but I'm kind of hoping we find some abandoned pot before we start taking apart the basement."

"I don't know. I'm kind of partial to the last time we were alone in a basement." I rub the back of my neck and glance over at her. "That doesn't mean I'm volunteering to go down there or anything."

Her breath catches with a smile and the world goes still around me.

And I feel something that is not total emptiness for the first time in weeks.

10

———

Nalini

I smile and barely stop myself from leaning in. I don't need to be seen making out in the middle of my future office space.

Not that it's not a tempting idea.

I clear my throat and step back, my palm resting on his chest for a moment too long.

"Yeah, well, it was definitely better than sitting in quiet panic in the dark by myself." I tip my chin, glancing at his wrists. "How are the tattoos?"

He offers his wrists for inspection. The dark Latin letters are no longer angry and lined with red. "Healing."

I run my fingers over the letters, not missing the raised flesh of a scar beneath my touch and the way he flinches when I find them. "Have you figured it out yet? Where you're going?"

Half of me doesn't expect him to answer. It's a deeply personal question that shouldn't be asked in the broad light of day without the shadows to help hide things we're uncomfortable with.

He offers a lopsided half-smile that's more of a self-effacing smirk. "Not really. But I'll let you know if I figure it out."

The door swings open, pouring in light and disturbing the dust. A large man who looks like he belongs in a biker bar somewhere near either a prison or outside of Fort Bragg walks in as if he owns the place.

His size isn't diminished by the bright turquoise T-shirt he's wearing that sports the logo of some marina in Florida. If anything, it takes a confident man to sport that color.

"You must be Nalini." He strides across the space and offers his hand. "I'm Bruce. I see you met Caleb?"

My hand is swallowed in his massive fist and I grip back tightly. I'm used to big guys like him. Some realize their own strength and adjust their grips accordingly. Others are insecure man-boys and try to show how much of a man they are by their grip.

Bruce is the former, because his grip is firm but not crushing.

It's telling. And for once, it's telling a good thing.

Some of the campus administrators I dealt with through the train wreck of the process of getting the yoga center on campus were crushingly insecure. They never realize a handshake is a dead giveaway.

"We've met before."

"Good. I'm working with Rossi Construction and Caleb's working with me and we're working with you. We're here to help with manual labor as well as keep you on track and under budget."

"I think Sam Rossi might be my favorite person in the entire world," I mumble.

"He's a great kid."

I smile because I don't think of Sam as a kid but Bruce clearly does. We're a generation apart. I wonder how different we look to him.

Does he see us destroying the world, as so many stupid think-pieces lament? If he does, he hides it well.

"Caleb is going to walk you through the schedule. I just got called for a busted pipe emergency over on another project. Let me know if there's any issues with the timeline or anything at all with the way we've got things mapped out."

Caleb looks as surprised as I am by the pronouncement but Bruce ignores his expression as he hands me his card. "This is my personal cell. Any issues Caleb can't handle, call me. But I'm confident you won't need to. He's our representative on the ground."

Caleb clears his throat. "Really? I can't even *spell* 'representative'," he says dryly.

"Well, I guess it's time you break out that fancy cell phone and figure it out. This is basic Project Management 101."

He slaps the folder he's been holding against Caleb's chest, forcing Caleb to either grab it or let it fall.

He grabs the file and Bruce leaves as quickly as he entered. "Is that dude always that intense?" I ask.

"Pretty much." He still looks like he's in shock and I'm trying to figure out why, other than that the job just got thrust on him.

"How'd you meet him?"

"He sort of dragged my ass out of an alley and forced his way into my life. He's apparently part of my stay sober plan whether I want him to be or not." He's moving beyond shocked, slowly, to something else that might be irritation. It was easier to read him in the dark when it was just us, than it is to watch a thousand emotions play over his face in the middle of the morning. "He's a retired sergeant major."

I nod. "That explains a lot."

Caleb sighs and opens the file. "Well, here goes nothing." He hands me a copy of the project schedule. "I guess this is the part where I'm going to pretend to know what I'm doing," he says, reading the sheet in front of him. "First order of business is we need to get this space cleaned out. Then we need to send in the lead paint removal team. While they're working up here, we can brace the floors and get that"—he motions to the hole in the floor—"repaired. Which, between us girls, I'm pretty happy to let someone else do."

I smile over my shoulder at his "us girls" comment as I walk over to a windowsill and lay my copy of the schedule down next to my files. "I think we can do this. How long does it take concrete stain to dry?"

He reads over the notes Bruce has given him. "According to the time estimate, it's done at night so we don't track all over it. Rinse in the morning. Is this the design for the entryway?" He tugs a sheet of paper out of the folder, showing the mandala design in deep gold-stained concrete.

"Yeah. Sam Rossi designed it."

"This Sam Rossi you keep mentioning sounds very different from the Sam I knew in the Army. This one sounds dreamy."

"Cute." I grin.

"Sarcasm is my superpower." He glances over at me, watching me intently.

"He couldn't have been that much different in the Army." I've known Sam for years and Caleb's comment strikes me as...off.

"He wasn't, personality wise. I just never really thought of him as drawing flowers and shit while designing building projects. He was our assistant operations officer and he was much more focused on applying a boot to my fourth point of contact." He clears his throat, his face flushing. "That may be how the story of the unicorn porn got started on a porta potty wall." He rubs the back of his neck and looks down at the file.

I try not to laugh out loud. "I was wondering what you two were talking about. Nice."

He flips a page in the folder, still not looking up at me. "I'm actually still learning how to be *not* an asshole so I've been avoiding things that involve—"

"People?"

He finally glances up. "Yeah."

"So does Bruce just always hand you things you've never done before and say go?"

He makes that noise again. "Yeah. I mean, he doesn't believe in a lot of hand-holding. And he reminds me a lot of my old brigade commander, who believed you get the most out of people by demanding more than they thought possible."

"Are you really doing this?" It's interesting; I've watched him take the folder from Bruce and step into a contractor role without even flinching. As though it's the most natural thing in the world.

He shrugs. "Bruce has threatened to hunt me down and kill me if I don't stay sober. And keeping me busy is apparently a good way of keeping me sober. And so seeing how I'm not quite ready to slip off this mortal coil just yet, I'm inclined to do what he says."

I smile easily. I can recognize the sentiment far too well from dealing with some of the senior NCOs I've met in the

Army. Sandpapery but doing it out of genuine love of soldiers. "Well, that's one form of motivation, I guess."

He glances down at the paperwork then back up at me. "And if I get to keep my hands busy around you...well, I think that's a pretty good use of my time."

~

Caleb

SHE LAUGHS. "Wow, you know how to make a girl feel special."

I like the sound of it. Deep and throaty and husky, like she's done it a million times before.

I wish laughing wasn't such a foreign feeling for me. I wish I knew how to be completely fucking normal around her. Around anyone.

"It's my specialty," I mumble, letting the space grow between us. I focus on the paperwork in front of me, then close the folder and glance around at her space. "So I guess the first order of business is to clear everything out so we can get the lead paint removal team in here. They're scheduled for Saturday."

I look around at the boxes stacked to the ceiling. At the tables and bins and remains of potting soil. "It looks like a lot, but tearing down is always easier than building up," she says. "The rest of my crew will be here in an hour or so but we can get started pulling everything out of here. I had no idea there was this much stuff left over."

"This looks like a lot more than just a pot-growing business." I pull my work gloves out of my back pocket. "The dumpster was being dropped off as I was walking in, so we can start sorting the trash from the things we can salvage."

She nods and pulls on her own gloves. "I guess we'll need to sort through everything and make sure that anything salvageable is, well, salvaged. I can resell it at auction or something."

I glance at my watch. It's just past seven a.m. and I've been up since three, unable to fall back to sleep. I wonder if this is going to help me sleep. I've done bigger projects with Bruce before but nothing like this. Nothing that actually *mattered* whether I screwed it up or not. "So you want to get started or do you want to wait for help?"

She shoots me a funny look. "Oh, definitely get started. Deadlines give me anxiety."

I'm not sure what to say about that. She seems so blasé about some things, tense and tight about others.

I look away, over at a nearby pile of tables—some look like old barn wood, others like they're pieced together from plastic and plywood.

"I wonder if Bruce would want the old wood for his... what did you call it? Maker Space?"

I frown and glance back at her. "That's the second time that you've said what I'm thinking."

Her expression softens and one side of her lip edges higher. "It happens to me all the time. I guess I'm used to it."

"It doesn't freak you out?" I follow her to a pile of boxes and she pulls a box cutter from her back pocket. I find myself wondering what else she has in those pockets.

"Not really. I guess it's not so jarring when you believe we're all connected at a deep level and sometimes those connections are easier." She slices at the ancient dusty tape in front of her, lifting the edges.

"That's a very Jungian perspective." I grab a broken pallet, lifting it to one shoulder. My bones protest when it connects hard but it's a good kind of pain. It feels good to just *feel.*

"Or it's a very Hindu way of looking at things. Jung pulled from Hindu philosophy when he was developing his theory of the collective unconscious."

"Really?"

"Yeah. It's only in the modern West that people are focused on individuals so heavily." She lifts out a bundle of baggies, held together by a rubber band. "What the hell am I going to do with all of these?"

"Sell them on eBay?"

She makes a noise as I take the first load of garbage out to the dumpster. The box of baggies goes on a flatbed trailer to be taken to storage. We work in silence for a while, moving trash outside in massive black contractor bags.

I lean one of the metal tables against the wall. "You've got a retail space planned, right?"

"Yeah?"

"You could repurpose these into shelves."

She steps close enough that I can feel the heat radiating from her. She tucks a strand of hair out of her face. "Can you do that?"

She glances over at me and for the first time, I notice tiny flecks of gold in the deep brown of her eyes. "Yeah. I'm discovering all kinds of talents now that I'm sober. Shelves are easy."

She smiles and damn if I don't notice her eyes drop to my mouth as I'm speaking. I don't step away. Being so close to her, it's a compulsion. A need I never knew I was missing.

Or maybe I always knew and that's why I drank.

I lick my bottom lip. I'm so fucking afraid of screwing this up. That maybe I'm misreading the situation and she's just being polite.

It's an easy thing to lean closer, slowly, so slowly. Giving her every chance to say no, to walk away. To put a barrier between us—a barrier I'm apparently desperately incapable of respecting.

And then she is there. Her lips brush against mine. Soft. Teasing. Just a whisper of a sensation.

Until she surrounds me, her gloved palm wrapping slowly around the back of my neck, drawing me closer. It's so damn easy to nudge her lips apart, to drink from her slowly. To savor the sensation of our breath mingling together, the slide of her tongue against mine.

"This could get complicated," I whisper when I'm certain I can breathe again.

Her lips move against mine. "It already is."

"I think I'm okay with complicated."

Now she smiles and I can feel it in the depths of my soul. "Me, too."

I'm here. In the moment. Tasting. Drinking. Feasting on her every touch, every sensation.

I'm lost in her.

11

───────

Nalini

I'm not big on regrets. I don't believe in living my life looking back, no matter how much I sometimes feel trapped by the past.

Kissing him was a risk. A joy. A touch of light after so much darkness.

My body is still humming from his touch. I've found ways to brush against him as we move in and out of the door. To be near him for no reason at all.

It's hell on my productivity. And there is still so much to do in order to get this down to a vast, empty space that we can properly remove the old lead paint from. When it's finished, it will be a wide area, capable of holding three hundred people. The main floor won't be just a yoga studio but an event space.

I take a long pull off my water bottle, staring at the dark hole in the floor. It's captured my thoughts, tormenting me with nightmares of what could be down there. Stephen

King's *It* scared the living shit out of me when I was ten years old and I've never really recovered from it.

Which made Iraq fun as hell. Walking through the maze of trailers to the latrine at night was a real trip to the beach. The crunch of boots over stone. The weird silence beneath the distant hum of power generators. The shadows moved and danced along the walls, bouncing with the light from the flashlight.

The stuff of nightmares.

Literally. I've found myself, time and again, trapped in my sleep in the terrors of that dark hot room where my life burned away and I was helpless to do anything but scream.

Caleb walks up, stopping close enough that our arms touch. "You seem awfully focused on that hole in the floor."

"I don't want it to be storage," I say finally. "Sam suggested that I rip the floor open here but...I think he's right. I want to open it up. To bring light down there so that it's not this dark nightmare factory where I keep extra yoga mats and mala necklaces."

"Those are the stuff of nightmares."

I bump into him for the terrible joke. "You know what I mean." I take another gulp of water. "The way he made it sound wasn't too complicated, depending on where the load bearing beams are in the building. Basically, rip that part of the floor out so that there's a wide open hallway running through this space. Put in glass doors and make two separate yoga spaces. One can be a heated studio. One can be a meditation room. It expands my options for classes... assuming things keep growing."

"It's a great idea." He makes a rough noise. "I was worried you were going to say we should start working in the basement and I was about to violate my no-drinking thing."

"That makes two of us." I grin. I shouldn't but I can't help it. "I'm avoiding the pit until I've smoked a lot of pot or gotten really drunk. And seeing how I've never really gotten into pot and I'm not a big drinker, it's going to be a while." I push my hair out of my face again. "So how much do you think that would add to the schedule and budget?"

"Well, considering Sam is the god of preparedness, he's got an alternate schedule laid out. It adds about three days, depending on the locations of the load-bearing beams. And considering that the two of us are too chickenshit to go into the dark and spooky basement to see what the structure looks like down there, I can't really say until we know that."

"Damn, you sound like you know what you're doing." I grin over at him, teasing lightly. "Are you sure you've only been doing this stuff a few months?"

He makes a noise. "I was in an engineer unit at Fort Hood. We built a lot of shit in Iraq and Afghanistan, only for the insurgents to blow it up the following week."

"Yeah, that pretty much mirrors my experience in northern Iraq and Syria," I say after a moment. I release a deep breath. "So everyone else should be here soon. Maybe we can summon some collective energy to go into the basement as a group or something."

He grins. "You're fine with telling everyone you're afraid of the dark?"

It's really hard not to lean into him again. "It's called humility. Admitting weakness is a sign of strength."

He makes a noise. "I'll try to remember that. Let me shoot a text to Bruce and let him know what you're thinking. He'll be able to give you a better estimate on everything."

He lifts the phone to his ear and moves over to one of the massive windows. I try not to notice the T-shirt straining across his back or the strong black lines rippling over his forearms.

But the black letters on his wrists catch my eye. *Quo Vadis*—where are you going?

I've never really thought about that question before. I've always been a little outside of wherever I was. I always fit the best after I left.

Except for West Point. I never looked back at that place and felt like I fit there. Funny how the Long Gray Line has tried to be a permanent part of my life no matter how many barriers I keep putting up to keep it out. I was so fucking happy to drive away from that place at graduation.

I've kept so very few people in my life from that time. I want to forget it. To forget what it tried to make me become.

I've never been back. I skipped the reunions. I skipped the Facebook groups and all the bitching about *the current corps of cadets has gone to hell in a handbasket.*

Some Old Grads have too much time on their hands. The current class of cadets are not my problem. And neither is the Army, for that matter.

I glance over at Caleb again. It's really hard not to notice the way his shirt clings to his skin. His back is broad, his arms thick. I wish I could remember more about him from that time, but then how would that shape how I see him now?

I've worked far too hard in my life to go back to the place I was as a cadet. To what the Army almost made me. He told me I was kind when he'd gotten in trouble. I don't remember being kind.

I remember being an asshole. Unsympathetic. Demanding. Telling the plebes that they were going to do degrading and demanding shit because, well, tradition and all that.

I didn't even recognize him during the storm. I've tried to

block everything out from West Point but sometimes, the memories come back.

And I am not proud of them.

It took me realizing what my company had become to pull back entirely. To turn away from the abusive subculture I'd become a part of.

It wasn't rational.

I watch him stretch one arm up the edge of the window. The way his back moves with the motion. It's a good distraction from the memories I'd rather forget. I'm not entirely sure I'm being rational right now, either, with the way my thoughts are derailing into a soft warm space where my body is pressed to his.

Priorities. Getting naked with Caleb is not a priority, no matter how much certain parts of my anatomy might disagree.

The storm has forced me to make a decision and in doing so, I've assumed a massive risk – not just financially. Everything I am is riding on this investment. On my fervent focus that I can make a go of bringing traditional yoga to a hipster college town. I only hope I'm taking the right lesson from the events the universe has sent me.

He hangs up the phone and slips it into his back pocket, then frowns. He pulls on his gloves and reaches down behind a box near the window.

"What do you want to do with this?" I have to look again. He's...holding up a dead rodent.

"Um, perhaps one should not be handling the detritus we find? Ever heard of hanta virus?"

"Well, are there laws about just throwing dead bodies in the trash around here?" He asks the question like he's asking about coffee or tea. It's so damn matter of fact that I have to wonder if he's trolling me.

"Not that I'm aware of. At least, not small bodies like that. Bigger ones you need to roll up in carpet and dispose of in concrete."

He tosses the rodent corpse into a black contractor bag, his lips creased slightly at the edges. "Well, that escalated quickly."

I turn away, letting the smile cross over my lips once I am safely turned away.

Dead rodents aren't exactly a dozen roses. I can't explain why it's so damn funny to me at the moment. Or what exactly has me shying away from the very emotions he's drawing out of me.

I need his help. A strong back and helpful pair of hands. As much as I find myself drawn to the smooth voice and strong hands and the dark ink on his wrists, I also need barriers.

I've worked too hard to let my hormones get in the way of good business.

Caleb

I THOUGHT I was used to workaholics in the Army but Nalini King takes it to a whole new level. By eight a.m., we've managed to get all of the tables sorted into what will be repurposed, what will be kept, and what's on its way to the dumpster.

We've got a long way to go before we're ready to start removing all the old paint but we're making progress toward getting everything stripped down to the bones.

I guess this building has hit rock bottom, too. I know the feeling. Looking around, I can see the potential that Nalini sees. The designs that Bruce handed me show the beauty this place is currently hiding. The high vaulted ceilings create a sense of majesty; the beams will support the lights so it's not dark and dreary. The high windows already let in a ton of light but when she adds window treatments the light is going to soften. Create a glow to the space.

She's got a plan and that's a hell of a lot more than I can say about my own life. I've just been puttering along, doing busy work with Bruce. Keeping my hands busy.

I drag a busted up pallet outside, tossing the wood onto the pile for recycling.

It's easy to fall into the physical work. It empties your mind so you're not thinking about any bad shit, or the burning need to take a fucking drink.

It's the kind of work that makes you sweat and collapse into a pile of exhaustion.

It's the good kind of work.

Not the kind of work that I'm avoiding back on campus with Professor Blake. I wonder what she'd say if I told her that I didn't want to finish grad school? Would she call my father? Would he even care at this point? The very idea of my father feels like I'm chewing glass—great bleeding slices of disappointment.

I walk back into the old warehouse, the scuff of my boots echoing in the silence. Nalini is standing near a window, tapping away on her smartphone, her brows furrowed into a faint scowl.

The light slants across her cheek, highlighting the soft contours of her face. A strand of liquid black hair falls from her high ponytail. Even in this moment of heightened focus, she's somehow hard and soft all at once.

It's strange, this hard twist of sensation sliding over my skin. Just watching her is pure pleasure. Like a caress of something electric and soft running over the length of my body.

I watch her then, knowing I'm supposed to be working. She looks so different from when we were cadets. God, but I hated her then. I hated everyone. Even Eli. The memory of so much hatred feels foreign now. But what does it say about me that I miss the anger that kept me going for so long? That the anger and the bitter little ball of hate in the center of my chest has been such a part of me that I'm lost without it?

It may have been a shitty way to live but at least it was consistent. Familiar.

That consistency is gone and the silence it's left behind is deafening.

I wonder if she knows what that feels like—to lose something that's defined you, even if that something was toxic and negative and utterly destructive, it was still yours. To turn your back on who you are and what you've been and try to rebuild when you have no idea where to even begin.

Looking back, I know why I hated everyone at West Point. It wasn't anything personal. It was...protection. Fear.

I don't remember when I started drinking. Or what it felt like before I lost a decade of my life at the bottom of a bottle. But I know what the last decade has felt like. What it's felt like to put aside the bottle and suddenly not be able to find the anger and the hate that had been near constant companions.

But standing here, in this moment, in the space we are deconstructing, she reminds me of the past. The past before I started to hate everything I was. The past before I lost myself.

She is a light.

Not a rope, pulling me along, making me go somewhere

I don't want to go. A light. Illuminating a path. A path that it is up to me to continue down.

It would be easy to walk over to her. To engage in pure physical contact.

I won't. I can't.

I'm in no place to even think about being part of someone else's life.

She swears suddenly and seems to barely avoid slapping the phone down on the brick windowsill. I try to move so it's not glaringly obvious that I was standing there, staring at her like some kind of stalker, but I'm pretty sure she's already caught me.

"You okay?" *Yeah, real slick, Caleb. Real fucking slick.*

"Yeah. The whole conversation you overheard earlier? Now they're playing the veteran card—asking me to get involved because my status as a veteran will give more credibility to the Wellness Center."

"Why are you irritated by that?" I tug my gloves back on. "I bet they give you free parking. You don't want your 'thank you for your service' military discount?"

It's a crappy attempt at humor and it falls painfully flat.

She shakes her head, her lips pressed into a thin line. "I have no objections to that at all. But the longer I've been away from the Army, the more I realize I'm not comfortable with the genuflection-before-the-saints-ritual that we do." She sets her phone on the ledge and pulls her gloves on. "It's not... I'm proud of my military service and I think others should be, too. I mean, if you want to change your Facebook profile to a picture of you in uniform every year. But I'm not comfortable with this idea that veterans are our nation's saviors. And using me to speak for all veterans is even more gross than using me as an Indian woman."

"I guess I never thought about it like that."

She shakes her head and lifts her phone before setting it back down, perfectly calm. I'm consistently amazed at how she can dial her temper back so quickly. "It's dangerous. To give people that kind of power and influence."

I frown then and lean against the table we're getting ready to move. "I don't see where it's dangerous. I mean, soldiers are taught to be leaders, aren't we? Why is it dangerous to get ten percent off at Applebees?"

She tips her head at me. "It's not the discounts. It's the… the idea that as soldiers we can't be criticized. The idea that when we speak, we somehow have more credibility than others." She motions toward the window. "On campus, they brought in this company to teach the yoga classes at the Wellness Center. Fine, right? Except that they didn't listen to the objections of the Indian students about how this particular company operates in India." She bites her lips together into a line that makes me cringe. "Now, they want me to come talk about how the Wellness Center can help veterans. And that's fighting dirty because I started my damn studio to use yoga to help veterans and…" She blows out a hard breath. "It's not harmless when people use their status as modern-day gods to influence otherwise well-meaning people."

"So it's the principle of the thing. Of them asking you as a combat veteran to endorse something to your fellow vets?" I brace my hands on the edge of the table behind me. "I've never honestly given this that much thought." I scuff the floor with my toe.

"Most of us don't and that's okay. But I…it feels dirty for them to ask me to do this when I can't support this and they know why. But they keep asking."

"That's pretty disrespectful."

"It's dishonest, honestly. I want to help our brothers and

sisters. That's why I'm expanding the studio to this space. I want to create a place where we can have meetings and events and bring people who are struggling to yoga. To help them. And yeah, I can't do that for free but I don't have to sell my soul to do it, either."

"What does a good project look like for you? I mean, what's not problematic?"

She reaches for her water bottle. "Research. Using yoga to help people. I mean, if people want to use their veteran status to sell T-shirts and coffee and whatever, fine. But all that hyper-masculine dude-bro bullshit is how we have a generation of veterans who either won't fucking talk about the things they did in the name of God and country, or those who won't shut the hell up about it and wow, this is apparently something that gets me really pissed."

She sighs hard.

"I was pretty much that angry vet-bro stereotype for a long time." I look up at her. "I was the guy who couldn't shut up about serving. About being better than civilians who never sacrificed." I reach for my own water bottle, to try and swallow the block in my throat. "I embraced it. Because it was the only thing that made me feel like I was part of something when I finally took the uniform off."

She presses her lips together again. "I'm sorry."

"Don't be. That's not who I'm trying to be anymore." I look down at my plain dark blue T-shirt, covered in dust. "I think this whole being-a-veteran thing is a lot more complicated than I realized."

She smiles sadly. "Yeah. I've spent a lot of time wrestling with it. Like how do I do this," she motions to the space around her, "and make sure that veterans know this is a space for them if they want, without doing the same thing that I'm complaining about the Wellness Center wanting me to do?"

"I don't know. Maybe it's got to do with intentions?"

She makes a noise. "Yeah, maybe. I think about Arjuna. When Krishna tells him it's his duty to fight. This place is my duty. To my Indian family and my American one. To those vets who find a place here. But that doesn't mean it's not complicated."

I tip my chin at her. "You talk about this place for veterans but...you won't have anything to do with West Point."

The question may end the fragile conversation. It may slap at her and piss her off. If I'd thought about it, I probably wouldn't have asked but the words are out there now.

"West Point. I don't like who I was at West Point. I don't like what I became. When I left and met people like First Sarn't Sorren and First Sarn't Washington I learned a lot more about taking care of soldiers the right way." She sighs hard. "I guess, their way of leading felt more right to me. West Point wanted me to be a hard ass, to follow these rules that only apply selectively." She straightens. "Okay. Break over. I need... Let's do some manual labor because wow, did this get intense."

She lifts one end of one of the remaining tables that still needs to be moved out of the way. "This is really solid."

I grant her the distraction from talking about the Wellness Center and West Point and veterans that clearly struck a nerve. I grab one side of the table. "It really is."

She stops in front of an old window frame that had been hidden among the tables. Standing there for a moment, she frowns, then lifts it up, testing it. "I bet we could strip this down and stain it. It might make a nice wall hanging."

I tip my head and try to see it how she's seeing it. Funny

how I could see the shelves taking shape from the old table but I'm having a hard time seeing this window as anything but a window. "It's just some broken-down old window."

She glances over at me and smiles softly. "There are always ways to find new uses for some old broken things."

I frown. "Are we talking about the window?"

"What else would we be talking about?" And just like that, the easiness between us fades to cool shadows once again.

A cloud moves overhead, blotting out the sun in the dusty skylights above. "I feel like that is a trick question."

She smiles softly. "There's a gel you can use to strip off old paint and stain. See this hole, right here? I can fill it with wood glue and shavings so it will take the stain. And it'll be good as new."

"Yeah but the hole won't take the stain as good as if you were to cut this half off and make it smaller."

"That's the point. You want it to look worn. The dings and gouges and scrapes in the wood are what give it character."

I'm a little unnerved by this conversation even as I find myself obsessed by her lips forming the word *wood*. Because I am fucking twelve years old, apparently. "How do you know all this stuff about wood and construction anyway?"

12

Nalini

"I like learning how to do things. Keeps my mind busy." Just like I'm enjoying talking to him. Working with him.

Watching him work. Because hot damn do his forearms make a woman think filthy, inappropriate things.

"And you don't like having an idle mind?"

"Not with an imagination like mine." I don't need to tell him about the fire or the way that it created an altar to itself that I'm forced to kneel before whether I want to or not. Every time I strip my clothes off, I'm reminded of what changed that day.

"I can definitely relate. The first thing Bruce got me to understand once I'd sobered up was how to keep my hands busy."

I make a noise as I stack the window frame onto the pile of salvageable wood. "Yeah. The mind-body connection is pretty strong. And it's sometimes a lot easier to keep your hands busy to get the mind to follow along."

He nods and drags one of the last remaining boxes outside.

I wish I remembered him more as a cadet. I would love to see how much he's changed. I suppose we all have, though.

"So I guess you don't like Veterans' Day?" he asks when he comes back in. He grabs one side of the last table and we move it to where the rest of them are waiting to be taken outside.

"It's not that I don't like it. I'm just...I'm conflicted about it."

"You have something against Freedom Cheesy Fries or Thank You For Your Service Buffalo Wings?"

I glance up at him and try not to laugh. "Are those real food items?"

"I have no idea but if they're not, I smell a themed restaurant idea coming up. I could pitch it to venture capitalists if I ever get my ass back into a classroom."

I laugh because the idea is so ludicrous. "Yeah, well, don't underestimate the need for people to wrap themselves in the flag and call themselves patriots."

"Is that what bugs you about Veterans' Day?"

"I don't know, honestly. I'm not opposed to it." We stack one of the tables onto another one, creating more floor space to be available for building the walls between the retail space at the front of the studio and the actual studios in the back. "When I first got back from Iraq, I was all in on the angry veteran stereotype, you know? I was pissed that people were making it about sales and discounts. That people weren't paying attention to oh, I don't know—a fucking *war* we had going on." I swipe my hand across my forehead. "But then, I don't know. I had time to reflect on it when I was in grad school. I mean, I think rituals are important; don't get me wrong. But I guess it just feels somewhat empty? Like it makes people feel good and that's okay and maybe it's important and oh man, I'm rambling." I glance over at him. "Sorry."

He's watching me quietly. Intently. Like I wasn't just running off at the mouth like a raging lunatic. "What?" I ask.

"Nothing. It's just really cool how you get all fired up about this."

It's my turn to frown. "I have never met anyone in my life that likes it when I get on my soapbox about anything."

He grins and tosses me my Leatherman from the table. I slip it into my back pocket.

"Well, you haven't met the right people."

We go back and drag another table off the pile together. "When I was a cadet, one of the ethics professors told me I was intimidating and bossy. That I needed to be more lady-like because no man was going to want to follow me or fuck me."

He flushes and says nothing for a long while. "I'm pretty sure he shouldn't have said that."

I clear my throat. "Yeah, well, I got over that a long time ago. And he was a she. So yay feminism, right?" One of the last busted-up tables goes into the dumpster.

"Did you say anything to her?"

A fourth table comes off the pile, revealing yet another stack of old boxes and pallets beneath. "What was I supposed to say? I was a cadet and she was a lieutenant colonel."

"You didn't tell anyone?"

I narrow my eyes and look over at him, pausing as we're about to lift the table. "You don't have any idea what it's like there for people like me, do you?"

"I don't follow. Aren't women in the military always saying that they're equals?"

I take a deep breath to unblock the frustration that blocks my throat. "Yeah. But that doesn't mean that everyone buys into that. And some of the old guard resents like hell that women—and especially brown women—are there and they're not afraid to let us know it." I pause as he lifts the other end of the table and we start moving again.

I start dragging again. This time he's the one who pauses. "So wait." He drags his hand over his forehead, swiping through the dust that's coating the tips of his hair.

"What?" I motion for him to start dragging again. We get moving again, heave the broken plastic table into the dumpster.

"Nothing. Never mind."

I'm not sure what he was going to say or why he stopped himself. I'm not sure if that's a good thing or not.

But I'm pretty sure I don't want to rehash all the fucked-up things that happened to me at West Point with him, on day one of a major project. I'm not here to unpack all the old memories I've been trying to ignore.

We go back inside. "I guess I see your point about Veterans' Day," he says after taking a long pull from his water bottle.

"It's not like I have anything against it. I just...Society needs rituals. So I'm not saying get rid of it. It's just that I don't know how I feel about it anymore."

~

Caleb

HER WORDS ARE the best summary of how I feel about life at

this moment. I don't know how I feel about it anymore. About any of it. Living. Breathing. School.

I don't know why I'm here. But I am...and so I'll make the best of it, I guess.

"I don't think it's a simple problem to solve," I finally say.

She pulls her box cutter out of her back pocket again. "I'm not sure it's a problem to solve at all."

"I guess that's a good point." I turn to the stairs leading into the basement. "Any idea what's down there?"

"No clue, but we're about to find out."

I pause at the top of the stairs. "If you need to change the subject, just say we're going to change the subject. We don't need to descend into hell to find something else to talk about."

She laughs. "Well, I'm pissed off enough to need something to do with my anger."

Jesus Christ, she's serious. I may need to start drinking again.

But I say nothing, instead grabbing the most powerful flashlight I can find from the toolbox and follow her down.

Praise Jesus, I find the lights. They flick on with a heavy, industrial buzz, flooding the space with artificial but deeply welcome light.

"This would be a hell of a place to hold a banging-ass party." The old stairs lead down to a massive storage space with a run-down stage in one corner. The ceiling is relatively high and the dust and the cobwebs give it a spooky, intense atmosphere. "Add in some illegal drugs and a cheap light show and you could charge fifty bucks a head to get through the door."

I spent New Year's Eve in Amsterdam one year. This space makes me think of it. From what I can remember, it was a damn good time.

She tucks her flashlight into her belt. Damn, she's like Inspector Gadget.

I lift open one of the boxes, shifting aside a sheet of yellow newspaper. A couple of cigar boxes are tucked into more newspaper. Inside, there's an old pipe. The handle is a glossy light wood and the place where the tobacco goes is bright, gleaming ebony. "Hey, are these anything you want to keep?"

She pads across the space. The moment she sees the pipe, her eyes light up. "Holy shit, yes."

"Is this good or something?"

"This is a Dunhill. They were high-end pipes made around the end of World War I." She lifts it out of my hand, turning it over in her hands. "This is really old. See this?" She points to a tiny stamp. "Our pot-smoking friends apparently had really high-end tastes if they were selling these."

I lift both eyebrows, rocking back on my heels as she tucks the pipe back into the case. "Okay, now I'm just dying to know how you know this."

"I was mildly obsessed with the fall of the British Empire after World War I for a while a few years back, and the impact colonialism has had on the world, especially India. I stumbled across these during a trip to Mumbai."

I fold my arms over my chest, utterly fascinated. "What kind of exciting life have you led that you travel the world, researching colonialism and old British pipes? That's not exactly a normal career path for a member of the Long Gray Line."

She smiles, lifting another pipe from its case. "Holy shit." She looks up at me. "These are potentially worth some pretty good money."

All told there are fifteen old pipes in the box and she

looks as happy as someone who just won the lottery. "How much are they worth?"

"I'd have to do some research but they could easily be a couple hundred dollars, depending whether they're authentic or not."

I nod slowly, impressed. "That's a hell of a score."

She makes a noise. "Yeah, well, just lucky we looked in the box before throwing it out, eh?"

"Guess we'll be digging through the rest of them?"

"Oh, yes."

She seems inordinately happy at the discovery. It does something warm inside of me to see the pleasure on her face. To see her eyes light up and her mouth soften.

If I'm not careful, I could get used to the sensation.

But that would mean getting attached. And I can't do that.

There are more heavy wooden planks stacked against one of the basement walls. "Why on earth did they have all this old barn wood and planks?"

She braces her hands on her hips. "You'd be surprised what those planks might be worth. People pay thousands of dollars for salvaged wood these days." She brushes her hair out of her face. "I mean, if I was going to open a marijuana shop, I'd want to draw in a wealthier clientele. Wood shelves, rustic décor would draw a hell of a lot of different folks than your normal head shop filled with cheap glass bongs and sex toys. Maybe they had bigger plans that got interrupted when they got busted. "

I cough hard. "Jesus, what kind of head shops have you been in?"

She laughs mercilessly. "You don't want to know."

"You know a very strange mix of people."

"Oh, yes. I know of one table made from the wood floors

of a Russian church that went for like eighty thousand dollars at a private auction." She grins, swiping her hair out of her face with the back of her hand. "Yeah. I'm pretty lucky like that."

It's hard to disagree. She's incredibly lucky.

She has her studio. Her passion for whatever this place is going to turn into.

I can't even begin to conceptualize what that feels like.

But watching her talk about the things she's done and the stuff she knows and the things that piss her off, I have a hint of what I've been missing.

Life. This must be what living feels like. Joy and sadness and anger and passion. All of these things in one package.

Once again, I feel a sense of loss for what might have been.

13

———

Caleb

We haven't made nearly enough progress by the time the door swings open and the rest of her people walk in.

I'll be honest. I didn't know what to expect from the people who work at the yoga studio with her, but I'm surprised nonetheless by them.

I smile and make all the right noises as she introduces me.

"Cricket Dawes was my right hand woman in the Army. She is now the goddess behind my marketing and social media, and is a logistics miracle worker."

Cricket smiles and grips my hand with a strength that is surprising given her small stature. She's tiny, with deep ebony skin and tight red spirals of hair held back from her face by a bright yellow headband. "Nice to meet you." She radiates energy in a way that is wholly enticing. I can see why people might gravitate toward her. "I brought donuts from Spike's Co-op. And Spike, by the way, wants first crack at providing your future coffee and tea shop with baked goods."

"You are truly a goddess," Nalini says. "I haven't even decided about a coffee shop yet."

"Yes, you have," Cricket says. "You just don't know it yet."

I slap my gloves against my jeans, watching Nalini's expression shift into a smile at Cricket's declaration. "Isn't Spike's Co-op a gluten-free bakery?"

"Yeah. They cut us a deal because we kept some of his specialty products in the coffee shop in the old studio. So, free gluten-free goodies." Cricket is entirely too matter-of-fact as she pulls the brown cardboard box out of a tan Arjuna Yoga tote.

I have to give it to Nalini—she's got her brand right: the archer silhouette is bent back, arrow pointing to the sky, surrounded by a blue circle. *Arjuna Yoga* is curved around the outer edge in crisp script letters.

The fact that Cricket is using the bags around town for errands—smart. Very smart.

I'm still skeptical about the donuts, though. I don't have any moral objection to gluten-free but I'm slightly attached to gluten myself.

I catch Nalini watching me. "What?"

"You look like you're about to gag," she says with a grin.

"No I'm not."

"You have something against gluten-free?"

I hold up both hands, knowing damn good and well I'm not walking into that ambush. "Nope. I'm just a fan of pure white flour and sugar, that's all."

Cricket glances over at me but says nothing.

"Shit," I mumble. I feel like an asshole. "I've heard Spike makes really great *kolaches*."

Cricket grins and folds the bag up. "I don't remember

the last time I had flour but from what I can tell, you can't tell his gluten-free from regular baked goods."

"Maybe I'll test that out later," I say, hoping that's enough of a peace offering. I'd hate to offend her thirty seconds after meeting her.

And holy shit, is that a far cry from what I would have done a couple of months ago. I would have run my mouth about how gluten-free people were going to be the first ones to die in the Apocalypse because of their bullshit eating disorders.

Bruce clued me in that being a dick about people's food choices was a really dickish thing to do.

I breathe in deeply, letting go of the anxiety that circles my heart thinking about all the fucked-up things I've said and done in the past.

"Bodhi's right behind me. He's getting the coffee and tea," Cricket says, pulling out what looks like the most glorious donut I've ever seen in my life.

On cue, Bodhi walks in.

He's *definitely* not what I expect. He's built like a brick shithouse. Okay, maybe a body builder. He's wearing a tank top—because who doesn't wear a tank top to a work site? Um, *nobody*—and is tatted out in full, bright-colored sleeves, one of which might actually be a peacock that spreads down one arm and probably across half of his back. His bright blue eyes are sparkling as he strolls in with a little too much swagger, and he's grinning from ear to ear like he's got a secret to tell.

"You look like you've had far too good of a night," Nalini says with a grin, taking one of the cups from his cup holder.

"I did. Graham and I went on a second date." His voice is deep and smooth and he is as far from being a yoga instructor as I can imagine. "I know it's your studio and all but I'm a pretty big fan of Mother Nature's destruction right now, because I didn't have to rush off to work."

He winks and offers the cup holder to Cricket, who takes one of the tan cardboard cups. "Who's this?" he asks, finally noticing me.

"Caleb," Nalini says, taking the lid off her cup and setting her tea bags in the steaming water to steep. "He's the site supervisor for Rossi Construction."

The introduction's only partially true—I'm here as a stand-in for Bruce. I'm not officially working for Sam's company.

I'm a fraud and Nalini just lied to cover it up.

I can't explain why that introduction rubs me the wrong way but it does. I nod and offer to shake Bodhi's hand once he sets the rest of the drinks down. "Nice to meet you."

"Likewise. You don't look like you're much into yoga," he says, gripping my hand with enough strength to break bone.

Oh good, a dick-measuring contest.

"I could say the same about you." I squeeze his hand back, then break the grip.

"Touché," he says lightly. But I don't miss the suspicion in his eyes as he watches me. "How long have you worked for Sam?"

"I don't work for him. I'm working with Bruce Forsythe."

Bodhi's expression shifts suddenly as he lifts the lid off a cup of coffee that smells like heaven from across the narrow space. "Oh, you're one of Bruce's strays."

"Bodhi." There's a warning in Nalini's voice. An edge that wasn't there a few moments ago.

Clearly, the dick-measuring contest has not gone unnoticed.

I straighten. I might be newly sober and I might really be trying hard at not being an asshole but I'm damn sure not going to get my punk card pulled by some vegan hipster. I've got some pride, after all. Not much, but I'm going to hold on to the last shred of it with everything that I fucking am. "Not sure what you're getting at, but if you've got a problem with me being here, we can discuss it outside."

Old habits die hard.

I'm either about to get my ass kicked or make a new best friend but apparently, we've got to sort out who gets to be in charge of this relationship.

God, but I am so tired of this dynamic.

I hold up my hands. "You know what, never mind. I'm going to get some air."

I walk off before I make any more of a mess of things.

Nalini

"Was that necessary?"

Bodhi tips his head, inspecting the contents of his opened coffee. "Yes."

I press my lips together in a flat line. "Care to explain why?"

"Bruce Forsythe has a habit of taking in men who don't exactly turn the right corner. We've all worked too hard to build up Arjuna Yoga without him bringing in some rando off the streets who might get drunk and crash a car into the wall." He sips his coffee.

"Care to elaborate what that has to do with Caleb?" I fold my arms over my chest, fighting an irritation that's mixed now with awkward gratitude for Bodhi's loyalty.

"Could be nothing. Could be Bruce has gotten better about who he brings on board for his company. *Or* it could be that Caleb is a train wreck waiting to happen and I don't want to see you left holding the bag because Bruce puts faith in people who don't deserve it."

It takes everything I am not to bite back at his judgmental attitude. The only thing that keeps me polite is the fact that he's doing it out of loyalty and protectiveness. Bodhi has that in spades.

"Caleb has worked hard to be where he is. I recognize that you're protective and I appreciate that. But that was uncalled for." I also don't need to tell him that Caleb has already been a train wreck. I have this irrational need to defend him in this moment. "I trust him."

Those words are surprisingly easy to say.

He presses the lid back onto the cardboard cup and says nothing.

Still. It grates that he's flat-out giving Caleb a hard time for no reason whatsoever. It violates my sense of fairness, even if it also triggers my wariness. "That's not who we are," I say quietly. "He's working with us. And until I have a reason not to trust him, I choose to trust him."

Bodhi presses his lips together and remains silent. I've known him long enough to know he'll take the correction without taking it too personally. He's usually so easygoing. It strikes me as wrong that he's pushed back against Caleb so sharply without even knowing him.

"I have to get something from my apartment." I stuff my gloves into my belt. "Start going through those boxes and seeing what's in there. We've had a couple of good scores already so don't just throw everything away. I'll be back in a little bit."

I head outside, stopping as Cricket follows me.

"What was that all about?" she asks.

I push out a deep breath then glance over at her. She's

been my friend since forever, since our friendship wasn't allowed because she was enlisted and I was an officer. "Just...I don't know enough about Bruce and his company to argue. But I know Caleb. And Bodhi was out of line."

Cricket folds her arms over her chest and I recognize the stance. "I'll talk to him. But you know he's just looking out for you, right?"

"I do. And I appreciate that."

A sly smile slides across Cricket's deep red lips. "You better get going if you're going to catch up to him."

I shoot Cricket a look, knowing that she's read way more into the morning's interactions than I intended. I roll my eyes and head after Caleb, my lie about going to my apartment thoroughly exposed.

14

Caleb

In hindsight, walking off the job site wasn't my best move. But Bodhi's welcome, such as it was, struck a nerve, reminding me that Nalini's space is just a work site.

It isn't my space.

It's funny how that sense of longing and emptiness hit me so hard at his words, reminding me that yes, I am actually a stray.

And yes, I have a history with Bruce.

I would probably screw things up eventually. With her. With Bruce. With everyone. Because that's what I've always done.

You fucked everything up.

It's so hard not to hear my brother's words. To hear my father screaming at me because I dropped a gallon of milk all over the kitchen. To hear my cadet sergeants hissing that I did not belong at West Point, that I was a disgrace for getting caught drinking.

Bodhi took one look at me and saw everything that I was. He saw the truth behind the lie I'm pretending to be.

And he called me on it.

"You always run off from job sites?"

"I needed to take a break." I glance over to see Bruce riding slowly next to me in his truck. "How the hell did you find me, anyway?"

"I was coming back to the job site and saw you walk out. Figured something had gotten fucked up already." Bruce parks and gets out, falling into step next to me. "You didn't sleep last night, did you?"

"That seems completely irrelevant at the moment," I tell him.

He glances over at me. "Yeah, well, certain times of year are harder than others for sleeping." He pauses and I get the impression that he's gone somewhere else, toward a memory where I can't follow him. "Like when certain anniversaries are rolling around."

I go infinitely still then.

The tattoos on my wrist are itching. Or maybe I'm just imaging things since they've long since healed.

I want to rub my thumb over them, but try not to scratch.

I swallow hard. But there are no words. I've been pretending that it wasn't happening. That I was fine. That this month was going to be fine.

"Anniversaries are particularly rough when you're trying to stay sober." The muscle in his jaw pulses as he grinds his teeth.

I open my mouth. Trying to find some way to deny the truth of his words. Trying to find something to say, to change the subject. Anything to relieve the terrible pressure gripping my throat. "I definitely don't need to do this right now. Not if you expect me to go back to work."

"I know what this month is, Caleb." He swallows hard.

"How?"

"I was the sergeant major of your mom's unit." He clears his throat. "I knew your mom, son."

In that moment I hate him. I hate everything that he is. Everything that he lied to me about. "Why are you doing this now? Why the fuck couldn't you just let me pretend to ignore this whole fucking thing? That was some minor irritation at the job site and you come and drop this fucking bomb on me right now?" I can feel my life unraveling. Like the thread of a sweater caught in a car door that's speeding away.

"It's been weighing on me for a while." He spits into the dirt. "I felt guilty about not telling you."

"Why fucking right now? This makes no goddamned sense. I don't need this."

"Because you deserve to know."

"Know what? That you're some crusty ass sergeant major who lost his whole life because he couldn't stop drinking? Because you picked me up out of an alley and decided to kick my ass if I couldn't get sober? I know all that. I know that the anniversary of my mom's death is tomorrow. *I fucking know and I was trying to fucking forget*."

"Pretending it's not happening isn't going to stop it from happening."

I lift my fist. I want to lash out. To hit him. To hurt him for dragging this up right now. Today. I was getting through. I was ignoring it.

I was going to be fucking fine.

And now...now I'm not.

I drop my fist. My eyes are burning. My chest is tight and I can't fucking breathe. "Fuck you, Bruce."

15

———

Caleb

I didn't go back to the warehouse yesterday. And today I'm paying for the sins of my manual labor, my lack of sleep. My back is tight and my hands feel like they're covered in blisters.

But it's a good kind of hurt. Not like the hurt that is still squeezing my chest and making it difficult to breathe. They say it's the pain that reminds you that you're still alive, right?

I haven't slept.

I haven't answered my phone.

I know what today is.

My hands are shaking. In almost four months of being sober, I've never wanted a drink as badly as I do right fucking now.

I drag my hands through my hair, pausing to stare at the tattoos. They still itch a little bit but they're mostly healed. *Quo Vadis?*

Where are you going?

My mom used to say that to me a lot. I wish I could

remember her better but she's fading. I have a few pictures of her in uniform. She's why I so badly wanted to graduate from West Point. Why I needed to be an officer.

But now, without my uniform, I'm lost.

I don't know what she'd want me to be. She'd be so ashamed of the man I've become.

Quo Vadis. I'm not St. Peter. Not by a long shot. Those words on my wrists are less about him and more about my mother's faith.

A faith I don't share. I don't think I ever did.

But that's not something I talk about anymore.

The alarm on my phone vibrates from the nightstand near my bed. I ignore it. I'm not talking to Bruce. I don't know if I'll be able to for a while. I tug a long-sleeved T-shirt over my head. I'm not ashamed of my tattoos but I'm not really ready for questions about them. Not today.

I can't even say what made me get the words carved into my skin after all this time. The dream I had about my mom a few weeks ago...her voice sounded so real. So close.

The words cover the self-inflicted scars from those first few years after she died, so I've got that going for me. I wasn't sure Vega was going to be able to make the tats work over the scar tissue. Guess I should have thought about that before I sliced open my skin once upon a crisis.

Glad that phase is passed. At least for now.

At least that's what I keep telling myself, anyway.

Sobriety isn't for the weak, that's for damn sure. If I can make it through today... My hands are shaking as I lock the door to my place and catch the bus to campus. I'm not going to Nalini's new studio today.

Bruce can fire me if he wants but he shouldn't have dropped that fucking bombshell on me. Who gives a fuck if he knew my mom? Who gives a fuck if he shares the same anniversary of her death with me? All of it's made me reach a whole new level of anger.

No. This isn't anger. This is rage twisted with sadness. I didn't need to know about him serving with my mom. It's not fucking relevant to my making it through today.

I swear to god if I don't get some coffee soon someone is getting shanked. Maybe if I drink enough coffee, I can pretend there's alcohol in it.

The Grind is my personal lord and savior on most mornings but today more than most, primarily because of the overall state of my body which, for once, is not hurting as the result of a vicious hangover.

No, this pain is all earned. It feels kind of good, if you want to know the truth. I haven't felt like this in years. Like I've actually accomplished something.

Which, to be fair, since I did not get up and immediately hit the bottle today, is also a pretty big deal.

Hey, even the little milestones count, right? One day at a time and all that. I can't even say what's kept me from drinking.

The Grind isn't very busy at the moment. Thank whatever powers may be for keeping the time between me and rage-fucking that cup of coffee shorter than normal.

No, I'm not really going to stick my dick in a cup of coffee. That would be weird. I may whisper something filthy to it before I swallow. Oh what, like you don't whisper sweet nothings to that first cup of coffee every morning.

Yep, I'm officially losing my mind. The coffee is bitter and dark and smooth. I lace it with heavy cream and dump a healthy dose of cancer—I mean sugar—into the depths of it.

My emotions are all over the fucking place today. I feel like a goddamned head case.

The coffee helps. It's pure, dark goodness sliding all the way down my throat and lighting up my neural transmitters like the hit from a smooth brandy, only without the important ingredient of...the brandy.

Hell, it's better than that. Not quite better than sex, but close. And given that I know shit-all about what sober sex feels like, I'll take my chances comparing it to drunk sex.

I head toward the library and the carrel I've reserved for exactly no reason except that I want to have a place to pretend like I'm doing some work for my degree. I'm lucky the woman at the admissions office likes me. Or maybe she just has a thing for soldiers...I swear I could have had a Mrs. Robinson moment or three with her.

If I was still drinking, I'd be tempted to try it, honestly. But sober? It feels...weird.

Not that she's not hot and all. She is. And damn if she couldn't probably show me a thing or two about how to tango, if you know what I mean.

Jesus. I need to go back to bed and try to be a human being again tomorrow.

I stop at the edge of the tech center in the library. Deacon Hunter is there, hunched over his laptop with Kelsey Ryder.

They're sitting close, close enough that his thigh is pressed to hers, their shoulders connected in a way that says more than graduate collaboration is going on here.

Something dark and green slithers through my chest, wrapping around my heart. They look happy. That new, fresh love kind of happy, but it's the kind of happy that you know is going to make it.

Deacon isn't a fucking Boy Scout like our boy Eli. No, he's got a wild side that came out to play one too many times over the last couple of years. I've pissed him off, too.

Wish I could remember what it was that I'd done. No way to atone for something you can't remember.

I turn away from them, unwilling to let them see me.

I do remember being a dick to Kelsey more than once. I may have offered to let her ride mine. I am not proud of that in any way.

But that's pretty much tied to how I started stopping drinking in the first place. Kelsey had always been pretty low key at The Pint, serving me drinks when Eli told her to cut me off.

But even then, she was off limits, and I plowed right through those limits one night after a few too many shots of Patrón.

A sick curdle of dread tangles with the caffeine in my belly as I approach my carrel where I've stored my laptop and all of my college work that I'm ignoring. The library lets me keep the space so long as I keep paying rent and they don't care that this is the first time I've set foot in here in well over a year.

I stare at my laptop. The coffee isn't strong enough for this shit.

But I'm here, even if I'm not yet willing to admit to myself why I walked into this room today.

I'm still sober by the grace of God. I might not be after this. This thing I have to confront in the bright fluorescent light of the carrel in the broad light of day – it might break me.

It's an easy enough thing to look up. To type in the words *Chinook. Crash. November 2003.*

My fingers are stiff, typing those words.

Then there it is: the War in Iraq headline from CNN. The Chinook got shot down over Fallujah carrying almost forty people, the deadliest day in Iraq since the initial invasion. The deadliest day since Bush declared major combat operations over.

I read the article. I read the list of names. Only one stands out. The only one that matters to me.

I read about all the ways my life ended on that day. About the way that so many other people's lives were altered that day because of a single rocket.

I can handle a lot in life, but reading this sober is harder than I imagined. I absently rub one of my wrists against the edge of my pants. The pain is familiar. Raw and tender. Reminding me that I'm still here.

She left. My mom left me alone. Once upon a time, I wanted her to be proud of me. I wanted to go to West Point because she met my dad there. Because she was an Old Grad.

I wanted to forget that today is the anniversary of that day. I wanted to avoid the pain and the sadness and the memories and everything that her death led to in my life.

I wanted to go to work today but Bruce—he fucking changed all that yesterday by ripping the scab off the wound I was trying to ignore. I wanted to keep my hands busy today so they wouldn't do something stupid. So they could distract my mind away from the ache around my heart.

I can't go to work today.

I can't be around people.

I sit and stare at the article on the screen. At the face of my mom, lined up with all the other pictures of other smiling faces lost on that crash. Captain Carmella Acardo.

She never took my father's name. I never knew why. And before now, it never hit me square in the gut that I didn't carry her name.

My throat is tight.

I don't know if I can get through today. I don't know how I'm going to do this.

But I need to figure it out. Because for the first time since my life fell apart, I'm determined to put it back together.

I don't want to be a disappointment to her anymore.

I just don't know how to do it.

I leave the carrel. Leave my computer on, the door locking behind me.

I have no idea where I'm going.

I'm sober.

But I am lost.

~

Nalini

I STUMBLE across Caleb sitting outside of my old studio. He's there on a stone wall, beneath a green-stained gargoyle on the Gothic church-turned-old bookstore.

I'm here to pick up some supplies to move them into my storage unit while the lead paint removal team does their thing over the weekend.

He's just sitting there, staring, seemingly unaware of the bright light of the sun illuminating him. Like the universe itself is making sure I see him.

I tried to find him yesterday when he left the warehouse. Tried and failed. I tried to hide my disappointment that I couldn't find him but I didn't do a very good job. We emptied out the rest of the space. If Cricket and Bodhi noticed anything was off, they said nothing.

Seeing Caleb there in front of the remains of my studio makes me feel a little bit off-kilter.

Something inside me calls to him, draws me nearer

when I'm not entirely sure his body language is something I can read. Or if it's something I even want to.

The supplies I need to move become a distant memory. It is Caleb I am focused on now. His eyes are bleak, his skin pale and drawn. The only movement he makes is to run his thumb over and over one of his wrists. It's a terrible thing that now I notice the scars I felt yesterday when I ran my fingers over the letters on his wrists. The Latin letters can't hide them now.

He looks up as I approach. He tries to smile and it falls flat and empty, and it's only a moment before he looks away. "I'm not going to be very good company right now," he says.

But he doesn't move. And I don't run.

"I've found that that's exactly when we need others around."

He swallows hard. "That's not always true."

"No, but it's mostly true most of the time." I sit next to him on the wall, close enough that my arm brushes against his back where he's facing away from me. "You really don't look like you should be alone right now."

He makes a noise that's somewhere between disbelief and telling me to fuck off.

I'm not sure which.

"You don't have to talk about it," I say quietly. "Whatever it is, you don't have to give it voice."

He glances over at me. Not really at me; more like in my general direction. "Are you supposed to be a therapist? Telling me that compressing things down gives them power? Like one of those sleeping bags that we ball up and stuff into that little black bag?"

It's my turn to make a noise. "I've never really heard personal trauma referred to like a sleeping bag, but I guess there's a first time for everything."

He's silent for a while and I let it ride. Sometimes, silence is what people need. To just let the thoughts tumble through the grey matter in our brains. To see what sticks and what doesn't.

Most people have a hard time with silence. We're social creatures. That social aspect comes with noise. But silence —silence breaks that human connection even as it connects us to something fundamentally bigger than any of us.

"How did you decide what you wanted to do with your life?" His question is quiet. Almost like he's afraid of how I'll answer it.

I don't reply for a long moment. It's not hard to miss the way he's leaning into me. Just a little. He may not even be aware of what he's doing but I take comfort from the pressure.

It fills something inside me.

"I needed help after Syria. I was hurt pretty bad and in a pretty dark place. I cut myself off from my family, from my friends. Everything. The fire... It took so much from me." I breathe in quietly. The memories don't hurt anymore. "I lost a part of who I was in that darkness. I didn't know how to be around people after that. And it hurt on a spiritual level because I have such a big family. But I couldn't do it. I couldn't bring myself back."

At least that's what I keep telling myself.

"One of the counselors at Walter Reed invited me to yoga. I refused. At first. I was angry. Frustrated. Everything hurt." Another breath. "I wallowed for a while. But then I started to feel the need for it again. The need for the movement. The need to stop feeling like a bucket of shit."

Now he's looking at me. Watching me as I tell the story. Watching me when I'm not entirely sure I'm ready to be watched as I go through the recitation that's become so rote as to become automatic.

At least in my head.

"You were at Walter Reed?"

I nod. "Yeah."

"You said you got blown up. You didn't say you were sent to Walter Reed. "

"Yeah." I shrug. "I got burned pretty badly in the explosion." I rub my hand against my right thigh, feeling the damaged flesh. "That's part of why I hate the dark." I swallow hard. "The burns got me sent first to Walter Reed, then San Antonio." I breathe out, deep, slow. "They're healed now. I can even feel a little bit of sensation in some places. So it's coming back. Maybe."

"Jesus, Nalini, I didn't know."

I try to make my smile genuine, but it's not easy. "I don't really talk about it. I'm not ashamed of it. But I'm not using it as my calling card, either."

"I didn't know. I'm sorry." He drags his hand through his hair. "That means the morning we spent in the basement...the storm..."

"It was an act of god that I didn't spaz out completely," I admit softly.

He lifts his hand, touching my shoulder. It's not gentle. Not hesitant. Strong. Reassuring. Warm.

"I'm grateful you were there," he says after a moment. "I mean, without the personal trauma and all."

Now my smile is more genuine. I rest my hand on his thigh. I'm not sure if I need the connection more or if I'm offering it to him. "That's the heart of it, isn't it? The stuff we carry around?"

I lean into him, shoulder to shoulder, the simple human need for connection. "I'll listen. If you want to talk."

16

Caleb

I follow her to her apartment, her hand threaded with mine the entire time. I'm not sure what I'm doing. I'm not sure what I'm going to say. It's all tangled up in my lungs and making it hard to breathe. But it's easier. To be here in her space.

Her apartment is small, overlooking the new luxury apartments near the Harris Teeter grocery store. Hers is not one of the luxury apartments. It's small and clean and tidy. Pictures of her family are scattered along the wall leading to her bedroom. Pictures that look like they were taken in India. Some in Maine.

She's smiling in all of them.

Her palms are warm as she slips behind me, her arms wrapping around my waist. "I have a big family."

"Is that a saree?" I point to one of the pictures with her and several other Indian women in brightly colored dresses. She's wearing bright gold and turquoise blue.

"Yeah. It was one of my cousins' weddings."

"It looks complicated."

She makes a noise and it vibrates through my back. "Draping a saree is a life skill that every auntie in India can do."

"Can you drape one?"

"Yes."

I turn into her embrace. Her hands slide around my waist and her head comes to rest against my chest. My arms slide around her shoulders but she is the one holding me. Her embrace is quiet. Strong. Warm. Filling me with connection.

With something as simple as a hug.

Part of me tries not to break a little at the well of emotion her touch has unlocked.

I clear my throat. "I meant to come back yesterday. I'm sorry."

"I was worried. And since I don't have your phone number, I couldn't stalk you to make sure you were all right."

I make a noise. "Are you asking for my number?"

"For purely professional reasons." I love hearing her voice vibrate against my chest, my throat.

I close my eyes, savoring the touch of her skin. The heat. The warmth. The pure human connection that's been so missing in my life. That I used to fill with drunk sex and obnoxious behavior.

"My mom died in a Chinook crash with thirty-eight other soldiers. Turns out, reading about it is a lot harder than just remembering it."

"Jesus." Her words are a whisper. Filled with horror. And something else I don't want to consider.

"And then I couldn't stop reading. About the war. About

the lack of armor when they invaded. About the lack of planning that went along with everything." The anger grips my throat once more, squeezing the air out of my lungs. "My mom died because we were stupid. Because our brilliant military leaders failed to plan. I've been reading about the thirty-eight people who died with my mom. And we sent them there, to be slaughtered. Why? Because some stupid politician lied to us? That's why my mom died?"

My voice breaks. I can't speak anymore or I might start to scream. The impotent rage is back, boiling. The need to drink is strong. Damn near driving me to The Pint, Eli's warning about not coming back unless I can stay sober be damned.

Her fingers are tight on my back.

I don't want this. I don't want her pity. I don't want the empty platitudes that are really the only answer to the futility of what we did.

I slide her hand off and push away. Going anywhere but here. Needing to get away. To get space. Air. Something.

I start to head for her door.

Her voice stops me. "Where are you going, Caleb?"

Her question cuts at me. Digs deep into old wounds that never healed. "I think I need some space."

"No. You don't."

I round on her, my fists balled between us. "Don't. Don't tell me what I do or don't need. Don't tell me I need to let this out and not bottle it up. You don't know what this is like. What my entire fucking life twisted into after she left me."

Part of me is horrified at my outburst. Shame crawls over me, hot pinpricks piercing my skin.

She doesn't back away. Doesn't flinch. Instead, she reaches for me, her fingers sliding around my wrists, her thumbs sliding over the Latin letters that hide the scars.

The scars I know she can feel.

I flinch. But I'm trapped. Trapped by the sensation of her touch. Trapped by the compulsion that needs the human contact.

"I wasn't going to tell you any of that," I say. She steps close to me, close enough that I can feel the heat from her body.

I close my eyes, undone by her simple statement. By her simple unwillingness to leave me alone.

She presses her forehead to mine. "You're not alone, Caleb." Her breath is warm on my skin. "And whatever sins you've committed in the past, you can't change them." Her thumb slides over my wrist, over the scars that are painfully obvious. "We all do stupid things when we're hurting. To try and make the pain stop. To try and tell ourselves that it doesn't really hurt."

I shudder as her thumb continues to trace the line of the scar on my wrist. The words start tumbling out, despite my horror, my shame. "My father sent me to military school when I was thirteen. He tried to raise me and my brother alone after she died but he couldn't do it." I close my eyes, the admission ripping out of me like a dam that finally pushes a single stone free only to burst from the pressure. "Boys at that age are cruel. I was small." I swallow. "I was a target. All I wanted was my mom back."

Her fingers tighten in mine but she says nothing. I'm not sure there's anything she could say that could be the right thing.

"I learned how to pretend the pain didn't hurt. I learned how to hide it." I swallow, the words like daggers in my throat. "I reported what one of the older boys did to me. I was bleeding and cut. And the sergeant on duty asked me if I was sure I wanted to report. So I didn't say anything."

She presses her cheek against mine. I feel the wetness on her skin. The tangible evidence of her ability to feel pain while I have long ago gone numb.

Her arms slide around me. Pulling me close. "You are not alone."

17

Caleb

I shouldn't do this. I shouldn't take this offering of comfort, no matter how badly I need the human contact today. A better man would walk away.

But I am not a better man. And the storm brewing outside matches the turmoil inside me.

And she is a shelter. Safe harbor beneath the rumbling skies.

I want to feel her pulse beneath my touch. Feel her body press against mine. Her eyes have never left mine. I'm intensely aware of the rise and fall of her chest, the rush of air from her lungs.

My body tenses and tightens, blood rushing to my groin. Her lips part, her pink tongue traces the inner edge before disappearing once more. I want to kiss her again; more than anything in the world, I want to touch her. To slide my fingers over her body, to feel her heart beat beneath my touch.

To feel her slick heat cover my fingers, my cock.

I'm aching now, my cock hard as steel. It's all I can do to avoid adjusting my pants.

Her gaze flicks down and I'm exposed and vulnerable. I can almost imagine what her skin would feel like against mine, how her ass would feel in my hands.

How her tight body would squeeze my cock.

I reach down, needing to move my cock away from the ragged zipper of my jeans.

She watches me. Watches my hand slide over my cock, watches me grip it. Christ it feels good, watching her watch me touch myself.

She's close, close enough that her breath mingles with mine. Close enough that heat from her body brushes against me. Wraps around me. Draws me closer, until her hand closes over mine and squeezes me, a gentle, demanding pressure.

I flick my jeans open, offering, hoping, praying that she'll keep touching me. That she'll stroke me until I can't see straight.

Praying that I can do this. That I can touch her how she wants to be touched. That I can find out what makes her squirm and what makes her scream.

What makes her wet.

The air is cool against my cock, her palm hot as she strokes me. Her touch is electric, sparks of jagged lust arching down the length of it with each slide of her palm.

I slip my palm over her waist, drawing her closer until her breasts brush against my chest. Her hand is pinned between us, her palm raw heat. She presses her cheek against mine, her breath hot on my skin.

"I want to touch you," she whispers. An erotic request.

She nips my earlobe, her breath a rush of sound and heat as she frees my cock from my jeans completely. "Say yes," she whispers.

"Please." She does that thing with her thumb again, sliding it through the moisture on the tip.

I've never done this. Never talked dirty with a lover. Never whispered the wants and the needs in the bright light of day.

There are so many ways that Nalini is my first taste of life after a decade spent as the walking dead.

Her hand moves faster now, gripping me tighter. She nips my shoulder and before my brain can fully register what she's doing, she slides down the entire length of my body.

She is on her knees, her eyes locked with mine. Her lips part and slowly, so slowly, she traces the tip of my cock with her tongue. Watching me watch her.

Until I fall away, tumbling into the darkness as she draws me deep inside of her mouth.

Nalini

IT's AN ACT OF TRUST, taking him into my mouth. Pure, erotic trust as I taste him. My entire body clenches tight as I lick the tip of his cock, moist heat flooding between my thighs.

I'm aching as I draw him deeper into my mouth, sliding my lips down his thick length.

When I saw him watching me, I knew, in that moment, that this was how we'd end up. With me touching him, burning for him. Needing to touch every inch of his body, feeling his skin against mine.

I suck him gently, one palm flat against his hard belly, the other holding him where I need him.

A little erotic thrill spikes through me when he finally closes his eyes and drops his head back, surrendering.

There is power—raw, intense, female power—in feeling him tremble beneath my touch.

His palm is warm against my cheek, cupping me while I suck him deeper into me.

And then he's urging me up, away from the pleasure I'm bringing us both. One hand cradles my hip, pulling me against him as he urges us down to the floor. The blue satin of my yoga mat is warm now against my bare skin. I don't know where my clothes are, or when or how they went there.

All I can see, all I can feel, is Caleb above me, between my thighs, surrounding me until every shred of my awareness is consumed by him. Only him.

I tilt my hips, urging him closer, urging him to press into me, to fill me. I need this, this reminder that I'm whole, that the scars don't define me. That the fire didn't consume my ability to feel.

His skin is hot against mine and I arch into him, practically purring with raw power.

His palm slides over my ribs, trailing lower toward my hip, toward the scars I know he can see but I'm not ready for him to touch. I thread my fingers with his, lifting our hands over my head. The movement pushes me closer, sliding down the length of his cock, feeling him slip closer to my core.

"I need you." A plea that's a whisper away from begging.

He slips his cock into my wet folds, sliding along my length. His touch is electric, pure thick fire.

He pulls away abruptly, rocking back on his knees and—praise all the gods in the heavens above—produces a condom.

I could make a joke right now about obstacles but it's not really conducive to getting me what I want—and what I want right now is Caleb, deep and thick inside me.

And then he's crawling over me, urging me to surrender, to lean back and accept him once more between my thighs. He's there, the wide flat crown of his cock brushing against my tight opening. He threads his fingers in mine again, lifting our hands over my head.

He's there, just there.

And he doesn't move.

It's an impossibly long moment before he lowers his forehead to mine. "I'm afraid," he whispers.

In that moment, I know what this has cost him. What he risks in being naked and vulnerable with me.

I cup his cheeks with both palms. Brush my nose against his. "Don't think," I whisper. Then I arch into him, using the angle of my body to draw him—finally—inside me. Just a hint, just the barest push of pleasure against my body that is craving the erotic friction. "Touch me." A nip against his bottom lip.

Please.

But I don't say that wanton phrase. This is too new, too risky.

Everything with Caleb is a risk. One massive backsliding risk.

But in this moment, the risk is worth it as he slides into me, thick and hard and full. My body vibrates as it expands to accept him. To squeeze him.

To...oh, sweet baby Jesus. His touch is fire. Pure liquid fire as he pulls out, then pushes back inside me. Striking the tinder until it bursts into flames, tearing the remnants of my soul apart and binding them forever with his.

18
____

Nalini

I'm surprised by how much I enjoy this—this quiet feeling of being skin to skin, the silence of our bodies touching, nothing more.

There's something about the silence between us. Something stretching and grasping, trying to form a sense of permanence in the impermanence of the morning.

"Tell me about why you hate West Point," he whispers.

It's surreal, lying in my bed, wrapped in blankets, cocooned within the warmth of his body. His question catches me off guard. "You really suck at pillow talk." But I slip my thigh between his, moving closer to take the sting out of my words. "What do you want to know?"

"You have this deep desire to bring yoga to people who need it. To soldiers. And yet, the very people who could help you—your Old Grad network—you seem to want to avoid. Why?"

He slides my hair off my neck and nuzzles me. It's a soft gesture. Loving. His need to touch is something I'm coming to expect from him. Something I could easily learn to crave.

I never thought I'd crave touch again, that I would trust enough to let someone else's hands roam over my body, my scars.

I'm surprised at how hard it is to whisper my next words. How my throat instantly constricts at even thinking about the ways West Point changed me. "West Point was the most difficult experience of my life. I was in company B1."

There are four regiments at West Point. Each regiment has nine companies. Each company is known by its regiment and letter. And each company has a different culture, a different legacy. Some companies have graduated more general officers. Others have had more of the goats—the person with the lowest GPA in the class.

Bravo company, First regiment had its own unique culture.

I close my eyes and inhale hard, deliberately constricting the back of my throat in *ujjayi* breathing. Calming myself as the story starts to rise up from the dark place where we put memories that we try to pretend didn't happen.

"Boys First was the motto." Another deep breath. "Well, they don't tell you that the girls who are assigned there sometimes are worse than the guys to other women."

But he presses against me. "When I was a freshman, the firsties bragged that B1 was the last company to graduate a female when they first brought women to West Point."

I twist my fingers into his, needing the support for my admission. "And I embraced that. I fucking loved it."

It's hard to say those words. To know that I embraced the toxic shit that said *other* women didn't belong at West Point. To know that I actively supported the culture in our company that led to the highest rate of attrition of females during my junior year.

That I thought I was one of the good ones. One of the ones who deserved to be there. Who could out-guy the guys.

No shifting blame. No blinders. No matter where this goes, I'll own it.

And I'll be grateful for moments like this. Moments that are open and raw and pure human connection. No matter how bad it might hurt in the future.

"What happened?"

I'm afraid to resurrect those memories. "There was one upperclassman. He was some big shot athlete or something. He was supposed to be the great hope that helped us finally beat Navy."

His arms tighten around me. It's almost as if he knows where this story ends.

"I was a yearling. My plebe told me he pinned her in a corner. That he demanded she recite some knowledge. When she failed, he punished her by making her low-crawl up and down the halls near the trunk rooms until her hands and knees bled."

"Jesus..."

"She told me what he did. How he stood over her. How he implied that he could do anything he wanted and she couldn't do anything about it. I didn't believe her at first." Another deep breath. "He laughed about it openly. About how he put that uppity little bitch in her place and I agreed with him. She should know the knowledge book. She shouldn't argue with him. She's a plebe and plebes are always trying to get out of shit. I heard him laughing with the company commander and the first sergeant." I breathe out deeply. "I watched my plebe start to fade pretty hard. I have no idea what made me believe her but I *knew* something was wrong." My breath is shaky now. "I turned him in. I went with her to report him for hazing. And the entire corps of cadets turned on both of us because he was thrown out of the academy.

"I was moved to a new company but it was still pretty terrible. Sam was one of the only people willing to still talk to me. I refused to go to behavioral health. So he gave me an order to show up at yoga the next morning." Another deep breath; my eyes are burning.

"Wait. Sam does yoga?"

I choke out a laugh at his attempt to make me smile. "Yeah. He does. I found my tribe. I made it through West Point because of the brothers and sisters I made in the yoga club. I became obsessed. Focused. It helped me. I know it doesn't help everyone. I know it's not a miracle cure that will magically solve all trauma and terrible things. But it helped me. It brought me back to who I was when I'd almost lost it."

He moves closer, if that's possible. Wraps me tighter in his arms. Pressing his chest against me, his thighs to mine. I'm completely surrounded. Cherished and held.

"I had no idea."

"It's not easy owning up to being an asshole," I whisper. "I thought I was doing what West Point wanted me to do. I thought I was being loyal to my company. I almost failed my plebe because I wasn't looking. Because I didn't want to believe one of my peers could threaten and harass someone else when they were good to me."

My heart doesn't hurt like it used to. I'm able to get the words out without feeling like I'm suffocating. It's amazing how things that control our lives for so long manage to look so different when you can change how you look at them. "I blamed West Point for a long time. But in the end, it's my responsibility for how I acted."

"There are good people there," Caleb says softly. "But a small percentage can do a lot of damage in the name of duty, honor, country."

He says nothing for a long moment. "That explains why you were kind to me when I got in trouble."

"Yeah. My firstie year, they made me a regimental sergeant major. Try leading when everyone hates you. It's not that easy." I feel her breathing, slow and steady. "I made it through. But I'm not ready to go back. Because I'm afraid that the person I was when I was in Bi wasn't an anomaly, but was a part of who I really am. And I'm ashamed of her."

~

Caleb

IT's hard to put into words how it feels when your oxygen is cut off, when your skin prickles with nerves and anxiety and anger.

Hatred for the person you were.

For the person you're trying so hard not to be anymore.

"That's not who you are anymore," I whisper.

"I know that. Rationally, I know that. But fear is a powerful thing."

She's an addiction. My drug. A human connection that I never knew I needed. But to know that she was part of that culture...

I don't have the words I need.

I slip out of her arms. Away from her warmth.

The cold is an instant slap against my skin.

I pull on my pants. Needing to get away. To hide.

To remove myself from her.

She sits up behind me. Her arms wrap around my waist, her thighs slip over mine. Holding me. Flowers and vines and lotuses snake down the sides of her body, intertwined in the scars covering her thighs.

She's a goddess. A goddess of rebirth and strength.

She's everything I'm not.

And I will never be.

"Where are you going, Caleb?" Her words vibrate into my back, her breath warm against my skin. "You don't get to do that," she whispers.

I turn my face, looking out into the storm as lightning flashes outside. "Don't get to do what?"

"Leave just because something hurts."

I laugh bitterly. But I don't stand up. I don't step out of her embrace. "You have no idea what's going on inside me right now."

Her palms fold over my heart and it's so easy to cover hers with mine. "People don't just start drinking as kids because they're healthy, well-adjusted people."

I want to pull my hands away, to break the contact. To staunch the wounds inside me.

The broken pieces of me aren't an excuse for what happened to me.

I close my eyes. Her voice mixes in my head with another one, until I can't tell where her voice ends and my memories begin.

I pull my hands away.

Turn away from the salvation I don't deserve. I look at her room. At the yoga mat in the corner, the tiny altar draped in prayer beads. At the pictures of her family on the walls.

A sanctuary. But the walls and the paint and the floors are only a building.

She's the soul of this space. The heart of it.

I can feel the burning of the tattoos against my wrists. Against my back.

"My father sent me to military school after my mom died." I stare at a painting on her wall, of a dark blue teapot with steam coming from the spout. I can see the lines knitting the canvas together. The way the colors saturate the fibers. "It was worse than B1." The shame crawls over my skin, hot and cutting, like steel through flesh. "I was thirteen. I'd lost everyone and everything that mattered."

I can feel the heat of her breath against my neck, an echo of the pain piercing my body.

I shudder. "West Point was a sanctuary for me. It was a place where I could finally feel like a man." I bow my head. Shame is cold and violent inside me. "I finally felt like I belonged. I got off on punishing those we deemed unworthy. I enjoyed it because for once, I had power."

She is silent, her breathing mixing with mine. It would be better if she left. If I tell the darkness, it can still judge me. It can still torment my sleep.

The nightmares are my penance.

"Nothing that happened to me is an excuse." My hands are fists by my sides. "I laughed when one of the guys told me how he'd made some of the female plebes cry. I was a willing participant because it hid the shame of what happened to me. I never spoke up. I never defended any of our plebes."

My throat is tight. My sins are real. Not pretend. Not wiped away.

"I've been a raging fucking asshole for years because I chose to ignore what happened to me before I got to West

Point. The same culture you rejected, I *enjoyed*." My eyes burn and my chest feels like it's being ripped apart by the violence inside me. "Because it meant I could pretend what happened to me never happened."

Her arms tighten around my ribs. Her palms are hot against my heart, like she's holding it together, keeping it from breaking out of my chest.

And I stay. Because I don't know where I'm going.

And for once, I have somewhere I want to stay.

19

———

Caleb

The air in my lungs collapses. I am a vacuum. A void.

Complete and utter emptiness. I want to speak but I can't. There is no force in the world that can force any more words past the block in my chest.

The air is rushing in my ears. I hear nothing but the static noise of the void. The darkness pulling me back, into the drink. Into the defense.

The pain is raw and cutting. The emptiness its own violence. Our shared toxic little sub-culture at West Point is one she rejected, one I embraced.

And then I feel her move.

The soft silk of her fingertips rests against my cheeks. Her palms are warm over the edge of my beard as she slips around to my lap.

"We can both be sorry for our pasts." She threads her fingers through my hair. I'm afraid to open my eyes. Afraid that she won't be real. That this will be a dream.

That I will still be alone.

"I can't atone for the terrible things I did. I can't go back and undo the damage I caused," I tell her. The words are rough. Tearing at my throat.

But they need to get out. I deserve the pain. All of it.

"No, you can't." She presses into me, sliding her arms around my shoulders. Moving her body closer. And I'm weak enough to wrap my arms around her, to press my forehead to hers. "And neither can I." She touches her forehead to mine. "Do you know the parable of the prodigal son?"

"I thought you weren't familiar with the Bible?"

She makes a noise. "I'm not up on the apocryphal stories but I'm familiar with the Gospels. There are myths that Jesus was familiar with Hindu philosophy."

I swallow, bracing at her words, afraid of where she's going.

"There were two sons. One who was loyal and stayed and worked his father's land. The other son was wasteful, went off and squandered his father's inheritance. And when the wasteful son returned, the father ordered a banquet and the son who stayed was jealous. He had never sinned. He couldn't understand why his father would embrace his brother who had lived a wasteful life." She presses her lips against my neck. "His father said that his first son already had his reward in this life. But that his other son had returned to him and he should rejoice." Her palm is a solid pressure against my heart. "Because not everyone comes back."

My eyes burn. The fire in my heart is something different now. Something...cleansing.

"You came back, Caleb. I never knew you before. I don't know the man you could have been if your mom hadn't died. Or if your father had been a better man."

I can't breathe.

"But you are here. You can't forget. I can't forget. And in many ways, the hurt I caused will still echo out through this life and the next." She nuzzles me, petting my side in a way that I've started to crave. "But you came back. You changed."

I don't know how to speak. How to respond.

The unconditional acceptance... "I don't deserve your forgiveness," I whisper.

"None of us do."

"How?" I swallow hard. The storm outside is mere rain sheeting against the windows now. The violence of it no more than distant flashes. "How can you look at me and know I enjoyed part of what hurt you and...still stay?"

"How can you look at me and not ask the same question? I ignored someone I was responsible for. I abandoned her when I should have protected her. I failed in my duty," she whispers.

I finally dare to look at her. Her brown eyes are warm and sad.

"Do you know what the hardest part of yoga is?"

I frown. "The pants?"

"*Ahimsa.*" Her voice is steady. She is the calm in the swirling violence of the storm inside me. That's not fair to put on her. That's not fair to put on anyone. "Nonviolence. Not just to others. But to yourself."

Her words connect, reaching the scared and crying child I've hidden from the world because he was weak. Because he wasn't strong enough to fight back against older boys determined to hurt him.

Because he wasn't strong enough to keep his mother from dying.

"We are most cruel to ourselves. When we refuse to forgive ourselves. When we refuse to let go of the pain and the past. When we refuse to accept what has been. The violence we do to ourselves is so much worse than what anyone else can do to us."

This isn't some rehearsed script. This isn't some speech she prepared for one of her classes. "You'll always carry the past with you. And it will still hurt." She cradles my cheeks. Her touch is a lifeline. "But you have to have the compassion to stop punishing yourself. To stop the harm you do every day." She brushes my hair off my forehead. "You can do penance until the day you slip off the mortal coil. But you don't have to keep hurting yourself. In that, you have a choice."

"I deserve it. Everything I've done."

She nods then. "That may be true. And you're right. You're not going to wake up tomorrow and magically feel like everything is better. Life is a journey and sometimes, we fall down. Sometimes we take detours off the path we thought we were on." She swallows. "I won't tell you that what happened to you is part of God's plan. I won't tell you it served a purpose. But for me...I am who I am today because of my past. And I am happy in my own skin. And I fight for that happiness every single day."

"I'm not as strong as you." This is my most painful admission. It hits at my greatest fear. The central part of me that is most vulnerable and broken.

"Yes, you are." She swallows and slips into my arms, pressing her body against mine. "I don't know where you're going, Caleb." She presses her lips against my throat. "But you won't have to go there alone."

EPILOGUE

Nalini

"You know I don't like surprises. And I hate being blindfolded even more."

The only thing keeping me from panic is the warm pressure of Caleb's chest against my back. "Trust me?"

"That's the only thing preventing me from freaking out entirely right now."

"Two more steps."

He's taking me into the basement blindfolded. It's honestly a miracle that I'm still standing and not hyperventilating. "Ready?"

"I have no idea."

He makes a noise against my back as the blindfold lifts away. The cool November air kisses against my now exposed skin.

But I'm no longer paying attention to the fear of the dark.

My eyes fill with tears as I look at what he's done. "Happy Diwali," he whispers against my ear.

I'm utterly speechless. The hallway is lined with small glowing candles, casting brilliant shadows along the wall and the double French doors that lead into one of the lower studios. Inside, though, is a *rangoli*—a brilliant painted drawing of the elephant-headed god Ganesh with small oil-burning bowls around the outside of the design. The studio is lined with small fragrant candles.

I smile as I notice one in particular at the center of the *rangoli* painting. "Is that the candle from the storm?"

"Yeah."

I turn to face him. I narrow my eyes. "I thought you said we weren't going to make the opening deadline because of the problem with the load-bearing beams?"

He smiles sheepishly. "Surprise?" He rubs the back of his neck. "When you got called to Walter Reed for that research opportunity with the National Intrepid Center of Excellence, I basically roped everyone I know into helping to get this finished in under a week. And I may have lied about the beams."

"How did you know I was going to get called to Walter Reed?"

He rubs the back of his neck. I'm starting to notice that's a thing he does when he's feeling...sheepish. I'm starting to love the gesture. "Maybe I, ah, reached out to my father, who knows some folks there. And asked if they were doing any research on PTSD and trauma and yoga."

The warmth from the candles caresses my skin. For the first time, the fire isn't frightening. It's not terrifying.

"You called your father?" The sheer magnitude of that effort...my heart tightens in my chest.

"It wasn't easy so, you know, you owe me later." He clears his throat. "He was just happy that I finally returned his call."

I laugh and step into his arms, hiding the tears in my eyes. His embrace is welcoming. Welcoming me home. Welcoming the light into the new space. "We're probably never going to be close. But he made some phone calls for me because I asked him to."

"Caleb. This...this is amazing." I nuzzle his neck. "How did you figure out about Diwali?"

"A lot of Google. A lot of reddit forums asking people how not to screw this up. Sam may have linked me up with one of your aunties back in India, who promptly called your mom, who made sure I didn't screw any of this up." He rests his forehead against mine. "She wants you to call her, by the way. She says if you don't, she's coming to Durham."

I lay my hands on his chest. The warm beat of his heart is solid and steady beneath my touch. He is solid. A rock.

I rest my forehead against his and close my eyes. "She'll come anyway, with my dad. She'll cook and you'll eat, regardless of whether you like spicy foods or not."

"Didn't you say she was a big time computer programmer? She cooks, too?"

"My mother has many talents. Keeping her daughter from going to West Point was not one of them."

It's so easy to stand here, in the light of a hundred candles with a man who has come to mean the whole world to me. Who knows my sins and who has touched my heart.

A man who has helped me stand in the light without fear.

A flawed man, but a man who has struggled to find his way.

His hands slip to my neck, embracing me. Holding. Simply connected, body, mind and spirit. I rub my thumbs over the black letters on his wrists. "Where are you going, Caleb?"

"I don't know. But wherever it is, I hope it's with you."

AFTERWORD

Dear Reader,

Alcoholism is not something I take lightly. Most people do not wake up one morning and decide to stop drinking. For those who manage to recover, it remains a lifetime of work, with many struggles and years of pain, both inflicted and experienced. I know first-hand the terrible scars it leaves on families. I know that the portrayal of Caleb's recovery is not typical and some may find fault with it. Research suggests there are two things necessary for recovery: first, a willingness to change; and second, a strong support group. Caleb hitting rock bottom was the element of change necessary to start on his journey of self-discovery and recovery.

In my research on yoga and trauma recovery, I learned that yoga and mindfulness is a way of linking thoughts to actions, and those actions can lead to successful recovery outcomes. In no way do I mean to portray yoga as a magic cure-all for addiction, but rather my intent has been to demonstrate the validity of scientific studies which support the efficacy of yoga and mindfulness as effective elements of a larger treatment plan.

Which brings me to the next challenge in writing this book. As I learned more about the spiritual elements of full yoga practice and philosophy, I learned more about the cultural history of India and why Indians, especially Indians in the diaspora community, are sensitive to portrayals of yoga that strip away the roots of the practice. Cultural sharing is a norm across human history, but deliberate erasure of cultural practices is a form of ethnic destruction. Some Indians are particularly wary of this due to a history of invasions and forced religious conversions in their homeland and within their cultures from the sixth century onward. My intent with this book is to portray the spiritual side of yoga that has helped me so personally while also portraying it as something that is fundamentally Indian in its origins. Most importantly, I wanted to show respect for the culture and traditions of the family and friends who made me and my family feel so welcome during our visit to Mumbai in December of 2017.

Any mistakes are purely my own.

Go back to the beginning...

Stay focused. Get a job. Save her father's life.

Beth Lamont knows far too much about the harsh realities of life her gilded classmates have only read about in class. She'll do whatever it takes to take care of her father, even if that means tutoring a guy like Noah - a guy who represents everything she hates about the war, soldiers and what the Army has done to her family.

Noah Warren doesn't know how to be a student. All he knows is war. But he's going to college now to fulfill a promise and he doesn't break his promises. Except he doesn't count on his tutor being drop dead gorgeous and distracting as hell. One look at Beth threatens to unravel the careful lies Noah has constructed around him.

A simple arrangement turns into something neither of them can deny. And a war that neither of them can forget could destroy them both.

THE FALLING SERIES
Before I Fall: Noah & Beth
Break My Fall: Abby & Josh
After I Fall: Parker & Eli
Catch My Fall: Deacon & Kelsey
Until We Fall: Caleb & Nalini

Note – these books are fiction. Any resemblance to real people or events is purely coincidence

The Falling Series, Book 1
Jessica Scott
Jessica@jessicascott.net
http://www.jessicascott.net
Jessica on Twitter
Jessica on Facebook
Sign up for Jessica's Newsletter

CHAPTER ONE

Beth

My dad has good days and bad. The good days are awesome. When he's awake and he's pretending to cook breakfast and I'm pretending to eat it. It's a joke between us that he burns water. But that's okay.

On the good days, I humor him. Because for those brief interludes, I have my dad back.

The not so good days, like today, are more common. Days when he can't get out of bed without my help.

I bring him his medication. I know exactly how much he takes and how often.

And I know exactly when he runs out.

I've gotten better about keeping up with his appointments so he doesn't, but the faceless bastards at the VA cancel more than they keep. But what can we do? He can't get private insurance with his health and because someone decided that his back wasn't entirely service related, he doesn't have a high enough disability rating to qualify for automatic care. So we wait for them to fit him in and when we can't, we go to the emergency room and the bills pile up. Because despite him not being able to move on the bad days, his back pain treatments are elective.

Bastards.

So I juggle phone calls to the docs and try to keep us above water.

I leave his phone by his bed and make sure it's plugged in to charge before I head to school. He's got water and the pills he'll need when he finally comes out of the fog. Our tiny house is only a mile from campus. Not in the best part of town but not the worst either. I've got an hour before class, which means I need to hustle. Thankfully, it's not terribly hot today so I won't arrive on campus a sweating, soggy mess. That always makes a good impression especially at a wealthy southern school like this one.

I make it to campus with twenty minutes to spare and check my email on the campus Wi-Fi. I can't check it at the house - internet is a luxury we can't afford. If I'm lucky, my neighbor's signal sometimes bleeds over into our house. Most of the time, though, I'm not that lucky. Which is fine. Except for days like this where there's a note from my professor asking me to come by her office before class.

Professor Blake is terrifying to those who don't know her. She's so damn smart it's scary, and she doesn't let any of us get away with not speaking up in class. Sit up straight. Speak loudly. She's harder on the girls, too. Some of the underclassmen complain that she's being unfair. I don't complain though. I know she's doing it for a reason.

"You got my note just in time," she says. Her tortoise shell glasses reflect the florescent light, and I can't see her eyes.

"Yes, ma'am." She's told me not to call her ma'am but it

slips out anyway. I can't help it. Thankfully, she doesn't push the issue.

"I have a job for you."

"Sure." A job meant extra money on the side. Money that I could use to get my dad his medications. Or you know, buy food. Little things, you know? It's hard as hell to do stats when your stomach is rumbling. "What does it entail?"

"Tutoring. Business statistics."

"I hear a but in there."

"He's a former soldier."

Once, when my mom first left us, I couldn't wake my dad up. My blood pounded so loud in my ears that I could hardly hear. That's how I feel now. Professor Blake knows how I feel about the war, about soldiers. I can't deal with all the hoah chest beating bullshit. Not with my dad and everything the war has done to him.

"Before you say no, hear me out. Noah has some very well placed friends that want him very much to succeed here. He's got a ticket into the business school graduate program, but only if he gets through stats."

I'm having a hard time breathing. I can't do this. But the idea of extra money, just a little. It's a strong motivator when you don't have it. Principles are for people who can afford them. "So why me?"

"Because you've got the best head for stats I've seen in a long time, and I've seen you explain things to the underclassmen in ways that make sense to them. You can translate."

"There's no one else?" I hate that I need this job.

Professor Blake removes her glasses with a quiet sigh. "Our school is very pro-military, Beth."

She's right. That's the only reason I was able to get in. This is one of the Southern Ivies. A top school in the southeast that I have no business being at except for my dad who knew the dean of the law school from his time in the army. I hate the war and everything it's done to my family. But I wouldn't be where I am today if my dad hadn't gone to war and sacrificed everything to make sure I had a future outside of our crappy little place outside of Fort Benning. There are things worse than death and my dad lives with them every day.

I will not let him down.

"Okay. When do I start?"

She hands me a slip of paper. It's yellow and has her letterhead at the top in neat, formal block letters. "Here's his information. Make contact and see what his schedule is." She places her glasses back on and just like that I'm dismissed.

Blake is not a warm woman, but I wouldn't have made it through my first semester at this school. If not for her and my friend Abby, I would have left from the sheer overwhelming force of being surrounded by money and wealth and all the intangibles that came along with it. I did not belong here but because of Professor Blake, I hadn't quit.

So if I need to tutor some blockhead soldier to make the powers that be happy then so be it. Graduating from this program is my one chance to take care of my dad and I will not fail.

Noah

I hate being on campus. I feel old. Which isn't entirely logical because I'm only a few years older than the kids plugged in and tuned out around me. Part of me envies them. The casual nonchalance as they stroll from class to class, listening to music without a care in the world.

It feels surreal. Like a dream that I'm going to wake up from any minute now and find that I'm still in Iraq with LT and the guys. A few months ago, I was patrolling a shithole town in the middle of Iraq where we had no official boots on the ground and now I'm here. I feel like I've been ripped out of my normal.

Hell, I don't even know what to wear to class. This is not a problem I've had for the last four years.

I erred on the side of caution - khakis and a button down polo. I hope I don't look like a fucking douche bag. LT would be proud of me. I think. But he's not here to tell me what to do, and I'm so far out of my fucking league it's not even funny.

I almost grin at the note. LT is still looking after me. His parents are both academics, and it is because of him that I am even here. I told him there was no fucking way I was going to make it into the business school because math was basically a foreign language to me.

My phone vibrates in my pocket, distracting me from the fact that my happy ass is lost on campus. Kind of hard to navigate when the terrain is buildings and mopeds as opposed to burned out city streets and destroyed mosques.

Stats tutor contact info: Beth Lamont. Email her, don't text.

Apparently, LT was serious about making sure I didn't

fail. Class hadn't even started yet, and there I was with my very own tutor. I was paying for it out of pocket. There were limits to how much pride I could swallow. It was bad enough that I wanted to put on my ruck and get the hell out of this place.

Half the students looked like they'd turn sixteen shades of purple if I said the wrong thing. Like look out, here's the crazy ass veteran, one bad day away from shooting the place up. The other half probably expected the former soldier to speak in broken English and be barely literate. Douche bags. Need to get working on that whole cussing thing, too. Couldn't be swearing like I was back with the guys or calling my classmates names. Not if I wanted to fit in.

I'm not sure about this. Not any of it. I never figured I was the college type - at least not this kind of college.

I tap out an email to the tutor and ask when she's available to meet. The response comes back quickly. A surprise, really. I can't tell you how many emails I sent trying to get my schedule fixed and nothing. Silence. Hell, the idea of actually responding to someone seems foreign. I had to physically go to the registrar's office to get a simple question answered about a form. No one would answer a damn email. Sometimes, I think they'd be more comfortable with carrier pigeons. Or not having to interact at all. I can't imagine what my old platoon would do to this place.

Noon at The Grind.

Which is about as useful information as giving me directions in Arabic because I have no idea a) what The Grind is or b) where it might be.

I respond to her email and tell her that.

Library coffee shop. Central campus.

Okay then. This ought to be interesting.

I head to my first class. Business stats. Great. Guess I'll

get my head wrapped around it before I meet the tutor. That should be fun.

I didn't think that fun and statistics going in the same sentence but whatever. It was a required course, so I guess that's where I was going to be.

My hands start sweating the minute I step into the classroom. Hello school anxiety. Fuck, I forgot how much I hate school. I'm at the back of the room, the wall behind me where I can see the doors and windows. I hate the idea of someone coming in behind me. Call it PTSD or whatever, but I hate not being able to see who's coming or going.

I reach into my backpack and pull out a small pill bottle. My anxiety is tripping at a double time, and I'm going to have a goddamned heart attack at this point.

I hate the pills more than I hate being in the classroom again, but there's not much I can do about it. Not if I want to do this right.

And LT would pretty much haunt me if I fuck this up.

I choke down the bitter pill and pull out my notebook as the rest of the class filters in.

I flip to the back of the notebook and start taking notes. Observations. Old habit from Iraq. Keeps me sane, I guess.

The females have some kind of religious objection to pants. Yoga pants might as well be full on burkas. I've seen actual tights being worn as outer garments and no one bats an eye. It feels strange seeing so much flesh after being in Iraq where the only flesh you saw was...

Well, wasn't that a happy fucking thought.

Jesus. I scrub my hands over my face. Need to put that shit aside, a.s.a.p.

The professor comes in, and I immediately turn my attention to the front of the classroom. She looks stern today, but I'm pretty sure that's a front. She's got to look mean in front of these young kids. She's nothing like she was when we talked about enrollment before I started. She was one of the few people who did respond to emails at this place.

"Good morning. I'm Professor Blake, and this is my TA Beth Lamont. If you have problems or issues, go through her. She speaks for me and has my full faith and confidence. If you want to pass this class, pay attention because she knows this information inside and out."

Beth Lamont. Hello, tutor.

I lose the rest of whatever Professor Blake has to say. Because Beth Lamont is like some kind of stats goddess. Add in that she's drop dead smoking hot, but it's her eyes that grab hold of me. Piercing green and intense. She looks at me, and I can feel my entire body standing at the position of attention. It's been a long time since a woman made me stand up and take notice. And I'm supposed to focus on stats around her? I'd be lucky to remember how to write my name in crayons around her.

I am completely fucked.

CHAPTER 2

Beth

It doesn't take me long to figure out who Noah Warren is. He's a little bit older than the rest of the fresh faced underclassmen I've gotten used to. I'm not even twenty-one but I feel ancient these days. I was up late last night, worrying about my dad.

I can feel him watching me as I hand out the syllabus and the first class notes. My hackles are up - he's staring and being rude. I don't tolerate this from the jocks but right then, I'm stuck. The rest of the class is focused on Professor Blake, but not our soldier. Oh no, he's being such a stereotype it's not even funny. Staring. Not even trying to be slick about it like the football player in the front of the class room who's trying to catch a glimpse at my tits when I lean down to pass the papers out.

Instead, our soldier just leans back, nonchalant like he owns the place. Like the whole world should bend over and kiss his ass because he's defending our freedom. Well, I know all about that, and the price is too goddamned high.

And wow, how is that for bitterness and angst on a Monday morning. I need to get my shit together. I haven't even spoken to him and I'm already tarring and feathering him. Not going to be very productive for our tutoring relationship if I hate him before we even get started.

I take a deep breath and hand him the syllabus and first lecture worksheet.

I imagine he's figured out that I'm his tutor.

I turn back and head down the stairs to my desk in the front as Professor Blake drops her bombshell on the class.

"There will be no computer use in this class. You may use laptops during lab when Beth is instructing because there will be practical applications. But during lecture, you will not use computers. If your phones go off, you can expect to be docked participation points, and those are a significant portion of your grade."

There was the requisite crying and wailing and gnashing of the teeth. I remember my first time I heard of Professor Blake's no computer rule. I thought it was draconian and complete bullshit. And then I realized she was right - I learned better by writing things down. Especially the stats stuff.

I look up at Noah. He's watching the class now. He's scowling. He looks like he might frown a lot. He looks...harder than the rest of the class. There are angles to his cheeks and shadows beneath his eyes. His dark hair is shorter than most and he damn sure doesn't have that crazy ass swoop thing that so many of the guys are doing these days.

Everything about him radiates soldier. I wonder if he knows how intimidating he looks. And then I immediately wonder why the hell I care what he thinks.

I'm going to be his tutor not his shrink.

He shifts and his eyes collide with mine. Something tightens in the vicinity of my belly. It's not fear. Soldiers don't scare me, not even ones who look like they were forged in fire like Noah.

No, it's something else. Something tight and tense and distinctly distracting. I'm not in the mood for my hormones to overwhelm my common sense.

I stomp on the feeling viciously.

I'm staring at him, now. I'm deliberately trying to look confident and confrontational. Men like Noah don't respect weakness. Show a moment's hesitation and the next thing you know they've got your ass pinned in a corner trying to grab your tits.

He lifts one brow in response. I have no idea how to read that reaction.

Noah

I had to swallow my pride and ask some perky blond directions to the joint. I hadn't expected Valley Girl air headedness but then again, I didn't really know what I expected. I managed to interpret the directions between a few giggles and several likes and ahs and ums. I imagined her briefing my CO and almost smiled at the train wreck it would be. We had a lieutenant like her once. She was in the intelligence shop and she might have been the smartest lieutenant in the brigade, but the way she talked made everyone think she was a complete space cadet.

She'd said like one too many times during a briefing to the division commander and yeah, well, last I heard, she'd been in charge of keeping the latrines cleaned down in Kuwait. Which wasn't fair but then again, what in life was? Guess the meat eaters in the brigade hadn't wanted listen to the Valley Girl give them intelligence reports on what the Kurdish Pesh and ISIS were up to at any given point in time. My cup of coffee from The Grind isn't terrible. It certainly isn't Green Bean coffee but it's a passable second place. Green Bean had enough caffeine in it to keep you up for two days straight. This stuff...it's softer, I guess. Smoother? I'm not really sure. It isn't bad. Just not what I am used to. Nothing here is.

I wonder if there is any way to run down to Bragg and get some of the hard stuff. Hell, I am considering chewing on coffee beans at this point. Anything to clear the fog in my brain. But I need the fog to keep the anxiety at bay, so I guess I am fucked there, too. Guess I could start getting used to the place. No better place to start with the coffee, I guess.

The Grind is busy. Small, low tables are crowded with

laptops and books and students all looking intently at their work. It's like a morgue in here. Everyone is hyper focused. Don't these people know how to have a good time? Relax a little bit? Hell, there were no seats anywhere. The Grind was apparently a popular, if silent, place.

The tutor walks in at exactly twelve fifty eight. Two minutes to spare.

"You're not late." I'm mildly shocked.

She did that eyebrow thing again, and I have to admit, on her it is pretty fucking sexy. "I tend to be punctual. It's a life skill."

"Kitty has claws," I say.

She stiffens. Apparently, the joke fell flat. Guess I was going to work on that.

"Let's get something straight, shall we? My name is Beth, and I'm going to tutor you in business stats. We are not going to be friends or fuck buddies or anything else you might think of. I'm not kitty or any other pet name. I'm here to get a degree not a husband."

My not strong enough coffee burns my tongue as her words sink in. She's damn sure prickly all right. I can't decide if I admire her spine or if it's unnecessary. Hell, it isn't like I tried to grab her ass or asked her to suck my dick.

The coffee slides down my throat. "Glad we cleared that up," I say instead. "I wasn't sure if blow jobs came with the tutoring."

She grinds her teeth. There isn't much by way of sense of humor in the tutor. She has a no nonsense look about her. Her dark blond hair is drawn tight to her neck, and I can't figure out if she is naturally flawless or if she is just damn good with makeup.

There is a freshness to her though that isn't something I am used to either. Enlisted women, the few I'd been around, either try way too hard with too much black eyeliner downrange or aren't interested in men beyond the buddy level.

But this academic woman is a new species entirely for me, and as our standoff continues, I realize I have no idea what the rules of engagement are with someone like her. At least not beyond her name is not Kitty and she's not here for a husband. Those she made pretty clear.

She is fucking stunning and I suddenly can't talk.

She clears her throat. "So are we going to stand here and continue to stare at each other, or are we going to get to work? I have somewhere to be in two hours."

I motion toward the library. "Lead the way."

Beth

He's watching my ass as I walk in front of him. He's just the type who would do something like that. The blow job comment had caught me completely off guard. I hate that. I always think of smart ass comebacks fifteen minutes too late.

So now I am even more irritated than I had been when he'd been staring in class. What the hell had Professor Blake been thinking?

I lead us to a small table out of the way where there wouldn't be a lot of disruption. Stats is one of those things that takes a lot of concentration. At least it had for me until I learned the language.

I pull out the worksheet from class. Homework and lessons. "So let's get the business stuff out of the way," I say. I hate the tone in my voice. I'm not normally a ball busting bitch, but he's set me off and if being cold and curt is the only way to keep him in line then so be it. "I'd like to be paid each meeting. Cash."

"What's your rate?"

I sit back. How the hell did that question catch me off guard? I don't know. I work part-time at the country club next to campus, but the tips are hit or miss. The thing about the other half? Some of them are stingier than others. Most of the time, I make okay tips. It's enough to keep the lights on most of the time. When it wasn't, I tried not to be bitter about how they didn't need the money like I did.

But I just smiled and took their orders.

I'm stuck. Noah is not my first tutoring job but my other jobs were paid by the university. I have no idea how much to charge for freelance work.

"Fifty dollars an hour, three times a week," he offers abruptly.

I cover my shock with my hand. "Huh?"

"Fifty dollars an hour. I saw a sign in the common area charging that much for Spanish. Figure stats should be at least that much, right?

My voice is stuck somewhere in the bottom of my chest. Fifty bucks an hour is a lot of groceries and medication. It feels wrong taking that kind of money, even from Mr. Does the Tutoring Come with Blowjobs.

"Will that be a problem?"

I shake my head. "No. That's fine." There's a stack of bills that need to be paid. The electricity is a week overdue. Like I said, the country club wasn't the most reliable income. I'm counting on tips tonight to make a payment tomorrow to keep them from shutting it off. Again. Between that and the money from tutoring - I could keep the lights on. I can feel my face burning hot. I turn away, digging into my backpack to keep him from seeing my humiliation, not wanting him to see my relief.

"Same time, same place? Monday, Wednesday and Friday?" My computer flickers to life.

"Works for me. How much pain should I be prepared for?" He sounds worried. He should. Professor Blake is one of the top in her field, and that's no small feat considering she came up at a time when women were still blazing trails in the business world.

"Depends on if you do the work or not," I say. I can't quite bring myself to offer him comfort. I'm still irritated by the blowjob comment. "So let's get started." I lean over the worksheet. "What questions do you have from class today?"

I look up to find him watching me. There's something in his eyes that tugs at me. I don't want to be tugged at.

He looks away. He's strangling that poor pen in his hands. Clearly, I've struck a nerve with my question.

I wish I didn't remember how that felt. The lost sensation of not having a clue what I was doing. I didn't even know what questions to ask.

I don't want to feel anything charitable toward him, but there's something about the way he shifts. Something that makes him vulnerable.

I run my tongue over my teeth. This isn't going well. "Okay look. We'll start with the basics, okay?"

I open my laptop to the lecture notes.

He finally notices my computer. "I haven't seen one of the black MacBooks in years," he says.

He's not being a prick, but I bristle anyway. "It might be old but she's never failed me."

"It can run stats software? Isn't that pretty intense processor wise?"

I don't feel like telling him that to run said stats

program, I have to shut down every other program and clear the cache. I don't want to admit that there's just no money to buy a new computer. I can't even finance one because I don't have the credit for it.

Business school is about looking the part as much as it is knowing the game so none of those words are going to leave my lips.

"It gets the job done," I say. "Now, the first lecture."

"I get everything about what stats is supposed to do. I got lost somewhere around regression."

"Don't worry about regression right now. We're going to focus on understanding what we're looking at first up. Basic concepts."

I look over at him. He's scowling at the paper. I can see tiny flecks of blue and gold in his green eyes. He drags one hand through his short dark hair and leans his forward. He's practically radiating tension, and I can feel it infecting me.

Damn it, I don't give a shit about his anxiety. I don't care.

"So the normal distribution is?"

I take a deep breath. This stuff I know. I draw the standard bell shaped curve on his paper. "The normal distribution says that any results are normally..."

Noah

She knows her stuff. She relaxes when she starts talking about confidence intervals and normal distributions. Hell, I can't even spell normal distribution.

But she has a way of making things make sense.

And her confidence isn't scary so much as it is really fucking attractive.

I'm watching her lips move and I swear to God I'm trying

to pay attention, but my brain decides to take a detour into not stats-ville. She's got a great mouth. It's a little too wide, and she has a tendency to chew on the inside of her lip when she's focusing.

I look down because I don't want her to catch me not paying attention. I need to understand this stuff, not stare at her like a lovesick private.

I'm focusing on confidence intervals when something dings on her computer. She frowns and opens her email. It's angled away so I can't look over her shoulder, but something is clearly wrong. A flush creeps up her neck. She grinds her teeth when she's irritated. I tend to notice that in other people. I do the same thing when the anxiety starts taking hold. At least when it starts. It graduates quickly beyond teeth grinding into paralyzing.

I glance at my watch. It's almost time for her to go. I have no idea how I'm going to get my homework done, but I'll figure it out later. I'm meeting some of the guys from the veterans group on campus at some place called Baywater Inn. Because of course LT put me in touch with these guys, too.

But watching her, something is clearly wrong. I want to ask, but given how our history isn't exactly on the confide-your-darkest-secrets level, I don't.

She snaps her laptop closed and sighs. "I've got to run and make a phone call. Are you set for your assignment for lab?"

"I'll figure it out."

Her lips press into a flat line. "You can always look it up online."

"Sure thing."

She's distracted now. Not paying attention. I watch her move. There's an edge to her seriousness now. A tension in the long lines of her neck. A strand of hair fell free from the knot and brushes her temple. I want to tuck it back into place but I'm pretty sure if I tried it, I'd be rewarded with a knee in the balls. And I like them where they are, thanks. I'd come too close to losing them to risk them now.

I pull out my wallet and hand her two twenties and a ten. She hesitates then offers the ten back. "We didn't do the full hour."I refuse the money. "Keep it. Obviously you've got something to take care of. Don't worry about it."

She sucks in a deep breath like she's going to argue but then clamps her mouth shut. "Thank you."

She didn't choke on it, but it's a close thing. I am suddenly deeply curious about what has gotten her all wound up in such a short amount of time.

Maybe I'll get a chance to ask her some day.

But I definitely have the impression that Beth Lamont isn't into warm cuddles and hugs. She strikes me as independent and tough.

And I admire the hell out of that attitude, even as she scares the shit out of me with how smart she is.

Continue Reading...

DIRECT FROM JESSICA
IBOOKS
AMAZON
BARNES AND NOBLE
KOBO
GOOGLE PLAY

A MESSAGE FROM JESSICA SCOTT

Dear Reader,

Thank you so much for reading. If you enjoyed the story, please consider leaving a review. Word of mouth is incredibly important for helping other readers discover new authors. I appreciate any and all reviews (whether positive or negative or somewhere in between).

If you'd like to make sure you never miss a new release, sign up for my newsletter at http://jessicascott.net/subscribe/ and please like my Facebook page at https://www.facebook.com/JessicaScottAuthor/. You can also join my reader room, affectionately known as The Pint for sneak peeks, giveaways and general all around shenanigans.

Until next time!
Jess

Jessica Scott is an Iraq war veteran, an active duty army officer and the USA Today bestselling author of novels set in the heart of America's Army. She is the mother of two daughters, too many animals, and wife to a retired NCO.

She's also written for the New York Times At War Blog, PBS Point of View Regarding War, and IAVA. She deployed to Iraq in 2009 as part of Operation Iraqi Freedom (OIF)/New Dawn and has had the honor of serving as a company commander at Fort Hood, Texas twice.

She holds a Ph.D. from Duke in sociology and she's been

featured as one of Esquire Magazine's Americans of the Year
for 2012.

Photo: Courtesy of Buzz Covington Photography
Find her online at http://www.jessicascott.net